# 悠 閒 自 得

## 中英文詩詞選集

—— 唐 清 世　著

# *The Epiphany of a Carefree Mind*

*An Anthology of Poems and Lyrics in Chinese and/or in English*

*By Chin Shih Tang*

# 序言

詩是我一生的嗜好。我對詩的興趣從高中開始，一直保持到現在。然而，直到1980年代後期我才開始譯詩。常常在課餘悠閒的時候，每逢偶然發現一首啟發靈感的詩，我就會試著將它從原文翻成譯文。練習用二種不同的語言，將意象以最逼真的方法來組合，令我感到興奮，而從事這工作所引起的喜悅是難以名狀的。

退休的最初幾年，翻譯的喜悅充實了我同時用中、英文寫詩的能力。使我感動的那些人生浮沉所掠過的生動情景，透過一已的領會、對源自深永意象的頓悟，以及對退休年歲的展望有一種新而微妙的變更—凡此皆有助於值得作為寫一首新詩的動機。借助對詩的長期投注，由是我寫了很多未經發表的詩，有原作的，也有譯作的。

近幾年來，我花了些時間，修改了一些可讀的詩，依類編組，結果有176首詩詞被收入一書，取書名為「悠閒自得——中英文詩詞選集」。

本書的主要內容，就如書名所示，概括了我一生嗜好的一些智力活動。

謹以此書獻給我舅舅，感謝他費心血扶養我長大成人，以及給順菊作為我們金婚之慶。

# Preface

To me, poetry is a life-long hobby. My interest in poetry started when I was in high school and has continued ever since. However, it was not until late 1980s that I started to translate poems. Often, in a carefree mood during my leisure time, whenever I came across with a poem that inspired me, I would make an effort to translate it from its source language into a target language. This exercise of associating images in two different languages with the utmost degree of verisimilitude excited me and the joys derived from pursuing such a task were beyond words to describe.

In earlier years of my retirement, the joys of translation enriched my ability to compose poems in both Chinese and English. Vivid scenes gliding through the vicissitudes of life that touched my heart, the epiphany arising from cherished images through personal feelings, and a new, subtle change of diverse outlooks towards my retirement years – all would go far to justify the motivation to write a new poem. As a result, a vast number of unpublished poems, original or translated, was worked out with the aid of a long-time devotion to poetry.

In recent years, I spent time editing some of those readable poems and organized them by categories into a collection of 176 poems and lyrics selected and included in a book, entitled "The Epiphany of a Carefree Mind - An Anthology of Poems and Lyrics in Chinese and/or in English."

The core contents of this book, as suggested by its title, epitomize the intellectual activities of a life-long hobby.

I wish to dedicate this book to my uncle in appreciation of the time and efforts he spent bringing me up and to my wife for celebrating our 50th wedding anniversary.

目次

序言　003

Preface　004


# 第一 | 雙語詩詞
（Bilingual Poems and Lyrics）

金婚吟　020

A Song of Golden Anniversary　021

歡樂無比：給Fred及Leia　022

Joys Beyond Words: To Fred and Leia　023

寶寶　024

To My Babe　025

「妳」的正身　026

The Selfie of "She"　027

詩人之專擅　026

A Poet's License　027

拾貝　028

Shell-picking　029

賣樂肯的從良婦　030

Malecon's Magdalene　031

晚年　032

Declining Years　033

分秒必爭　032

Beating the Clock　033

邂逅　034

An Encounter　035

祝您生日快樂　036

Happy Birthday to You　037

今天　036

Today　037

賀友人九十大壽　038

In Celebration of a Friend's Ninetieth Birthday　039

赤子心　038

A Naked Mind　039

基地之前廳　040

A Hall to Graveyard　041

孤雁　042

A Lone Goose　043

懷念　044

Reminiscence　045

闊別　044

A Long Hiatus　045

賞鬱金香　046

Adoring Tulips　047

一事無成　048

Nothing Accomplished　049

# 第一 中文詩詞

（Poems and Lyrics Composed in Chinese）

媽的諾言　052

秋色繽紛　054

安養院263室的病人　055

庵寺怨　056

祝壽有感　056

憶亡夫　057

友人八十大壽有感　057

更漏子　058

長生嘆　058

太平島塔燈修竣有感　058

故宅　059

遊黃山有感　059

安養院的老人　059

遊織金洞有感　060

黯鄉魂　060

灑脫　061

人性　061

菩薩蠻　061

晨起獨白　062

老來嘆　062

# 第三 英詩
(Poems Composed in English)

To My Other Father　064

To Our Dearest Leia　065

To Larry and Melissa　066

In Memory of the God-Man　067

Why I Want to Know Him More?　067

Grasp Without Reach?　068

Atonement　069

The Sound of Silence in a Nursing Home　069

Second to None?　070

The Innocent　070

Class Reunion　071

The True Color of Lies　071

Politicians' Gimmick　072

Doctor-assisted Death　073

A Living Stone Without a Soul　073

The Man Who Spoils His Boss at Home　074

The Specter of Death　075

Crib Death　076

The Irony of Excitement　077

A Short Visit　078

# 第四 中詩（詞）英譯
（Poems and Lyrics Translated from Chinese into English）

詩經・周南・桃夭　080

The Book of Songs · Odes of Zhou and South · The Tào-yāo　081

詩經・邶風・靜女　082

The Book of Songs · Odes of Bei · The Jing-nǚ　083

秋風辭　劉徹　084

The Words of Autumn Wind　Liu Chè　085

詠懷　阮籍　084

Exposition of Feelings　Ruǎn Ji　085

飲酒（第七首）　陶淵明　086

Drinking Wine (No. 7)　Táo Yuān-ming　087

飲酒（第十三首）　陶淵明　088

Drinking Wine (No. 13)　Táo Yuān-ming　089

敦煌曲子詞集・傾杯樂　090

Dunhuang Quziciji · Ch'ing-pei lo　091

渡漢江　宋之問　092

Crossing the Hàn River　Song Zhi-wen　093

渭城曲　王維　092

A Song at Wèi Chéng　Wang Wei　093

鹿柴　王維　094

Lù Chái　Wang Wei　095

哥舒歌　西鄙人　094

A Song in Honor of General Gēshū　Author Unknown　095

越中覽古　李白　096

Touring the Relics in the Middle Land of the Yuè　Li Po　097

菩薩蠻　李白　096

Pú-sà mán　Li Po　097

月下獨酌　李白　098

Drinking Alone in Moonlight　Li Po　099

春日醉起言志　李白　100

Life Perceived After Waking up from a Drink in Springtime
　　Li Po　101

春日憶李白　杜甫　102

Thinking of Li Po on a Spring Day　Dù Fǔ　103

畫鷹　杜甫　102

A Painted Hawk　Dù Fǔ　103

怨詩　孟郊　104

A Poem of Despair　Mèng Jiāo　105

問劉十九　劉禹錫　104

An Invitation to Liú Shíjiǔ　Liú Yǔ-xī　105

浪濤沙　劉禹錫　106

Làng-tāo shà　Liú Yǔ-xī　107

戲贈友人　賈島　106

To a Friend for Fun　Jiǎ Dǎo　107

送人東遊　溫庭筠　108

Seeing a Friend off to the EastWēn Ting-jūn　109

更漏子（一）　溫庭筠　110

Gèng-lòu zì (No. 1)　Wēn Ting-jūn　111

更漏子（二）　溫庭筠　112

Gèng-lòu zì (No. 2)　Wēn Ting-jūn　113

更漏子（三）　溫庭筠　114

Gèng-lòu zì (No. 3)　Wēn Ting-jūn　115

更漏子（四）　溫庭筠　116

Gèng-lòu zì (No. 4)　Wēn Ting-jūn　117

菩薩蠻（一）　溫庭筠　118

Pú-sà mán (No. 1)　Wēn Ting-jūn　119

菩薩蠻（二）　溫庭筠　118

Pú-sà mán (No. 2)　Wēn Ting-jūn　119

商山早行　溫庭筠　120

Morning Departure from Mountain Shāng　Wēn Ting-jūn　121

無題　李商隱　120

Untitled　Lǐ Shāng-yǐn　121

寄令狐郎中　李商隱　122

A Message to Official Līng Hú　Lǐ Shāng-yǐn　123

落花　李商隱　122

Falling Flowers　Lǐ Shāng-yǐn　123

嫦娥　李商隱　124

The Moon Goddess　Lǐ Shāng-yǐn　125

無題（一）　李商隱　124

Untitled (No. 1)　Lǐ Shāng-yǐn　125

無題（二）　李商隱　126

Untitled (No. 2)　Lǐ Shāng-yǐn　127

無題（三）　李商隱　126

Untitled (No. 3)　Lǐ Shāng-yǐn　127

無題（四）　李商隱　128

Untitled (No. 4)　Lǐ Shāng-yǐn　129

無題（五）　李商隱　128

Untitled (No.5)　Lǐ Shāng-yǐn　129

瑤池　李商隱　130

The Jasper Lake Fairyland　Lǐ Shāng-yǐn　131

賈生　李商隱　130

The Scholar Jiǎ　Lǐ Shāng-yǐn　131

蟬　李商隱　132

Cicada　Lǐ Shāng-yǐn　133

籌筆驛　李商隱　132

A Marshal's Posthouse　Lǐ Shāng-yǐn　133

錦瑟　李商隱　134

A Luxurious Zither　Lǐ Shāng-yǐn　135

為有　李商隱　134

Lest He Misses Her　Lǐ Shāng-yǐn　135

春雨　李商隱　136

Rain in Spring　Lǐ Shāng-yǐn　137

涼思　李商隱　136

A Woeful Thought　Lǐ Shāng-yǐn　137

風雨　李商隱　138

Rain in the Wind　Lǐ Shāng-yǐn　139

隋宮（一）　李商隱　140

The Suí's Palace (No. 1)　Lǐ Shāng-yǐn　141

隋宮（二）　李商隱　140

The Suí's Palace (No. 2)　Lǐ Shāng-yǐn　141

北青蘿　李商隱　142

To a Green-vine Hut in North　Lǐ Shāng-yǐn　143

登樂遊原　李商隱　142

A Ride to an Ancient Tomb　Lǐ Shāng-yǐn　143

宮詞　薛逢　144

A Palace Poem　Xuē Féng　145

灞上秋居　馬戴　144

Autumn Life at Bà Plain　Mǎ Dài　145

馬嵬坡　鄭畋　146

Mǎ Wēi Pō　Zhèng Tián　147

菩薩蠻（詞組五首）　韋莊　148

Pú-sà mán (No.1-No.5)　Wéi Zhuāng　149

女冠子　韋莊　152

Nǚ-guàn zì　Wéi Zhuāng　153

章台夜思　韋莊　154

Brooding at Night in Terrace Tower　Wéi Zhuāng　155

金陵圖　韋莊　154

A Bird's-eye View of Jinling　Wéi Zhuāng　155

書邊事　張喬　156

Recording Frontier Affairs　Zhāng Qiáo　157

已涼　韓偓　156

The Crept-in Cold　Hán Wò　157

春怨　金昌緒　158

Blues in Spring　īn Chāng-xú　159

春宮怨　杜荀鶴　158

A Palace-lady's Grudge in Spring　Dù Xún-hè　159

除夜有作　崔塗　160

A Note on New Year's Eve　Cuī Tú　161

貧女　秦韜玉　160

A Destitute Girl　Qín Tāo-yù　161

寄人　張泌　162

A Note to You　Zhāng Mì　163

菩薩蠻　無名氏　162

Pú-sà mán　Author Unknown　163

雜詩　無名氏　164

An Ad-lib Poem　Author Unknown　165

鵲踏枝　馮延巳　164

Què-tà zhī　Féng Yán-sì　165

相見歡　李煜　166

Xiàng-jiàn huān　Lǐ Yù　167

虞美人　李煜　166

Yú-měi yén　Lǐ Yù　167

浪濤沙　李煜　168

Làng-tāo shā　Lǐ Yù　169

破陣子　李煜　168

Pò-zhèn zì　Lǐ Yù　169

渡中江望石城淚下　李煜　170

Gazing in Tears at the Stone City, While Crossing the River

　　Lǐ Yù　171

相見歡　李煜　170

Xiàng-jiàn huān　Lǐ Yù　171

浣溪沙　李煜　172

Huàn-xī shà　Lǐ Yù　173

一斛珠　李煜　172

Yī-hú zhū　Lǐ Yù　173

菩薩蠻（一）　李煜　174

Pú-sà mán (No.1)　Lǐ Yù　175

菩薩蠻（二）　李煜　174

Pú-sà mán (No.2)　Lǐ Yù　175

菩薩蠻（三）李煜　176

Pú-sà mán (No.3)　Lǐ Yù　177

浣溪沙　李璟　178

Huàn-xī shà　Lǐ Jǐng　179

定風波　柳永　180

Dìng-fēng bō　Liǔ Yǎng　181

滿江紅　柳永　182

Mân-jiān hóng　Liǔ Yǎng　183

雨霖鈴　柳永　184

Yù-lín líng　Liǔ Yǎng　185

八聲甘州　柳永　186

Bā-shēn gān-zhōu　Liǔ Yǎng　187

夜半樂　柳永　188

Yè-bàn lè　Liǔ Yǎng　189

戚氏　柳永　192

Qī-shì　Liǔ Yǎng　193

歸朝歡　柳永　198

Guī-cháo huān　Liǔ Yǎng　199

鬻鹽歌　柳永　200

A Song of Sea-water Brewers　Liǔ Yǎng　201

蝶戀花　歐陽修　206

Dié-liàn huā　Ōu-Yang Xiū　207

杏花　王安石　206

An Apricot Flower　Wáng Ān-shí　207

江城子　蘇軾　208

Jiāng-chéng zì　Sū Shì　209

送鄭戶曹　蘇軾　210

Seeing off Financial Officer Zhèng　Sū Shì　211

寄子由（摘自中秋月寄子由三首）　蘇軾　214

To Zǐ Yó　Sū Shì　215

紅梅　蘇軾　216

Red Plum　Sū Shì　217

木蘭花令　蘇軾　216

Mù-lán huā-lìng　Sū Shì　217

念奴嬌　蘇軾　218

Niàn-nú jiāo　Sū Shì　219

水調歌頭　蘇軾　220

Shuǐ-diào gē-tóu　Sū Shì　221

水龍吟　蘇軾　222

Shuǐ-lóng yín　Sū Shì　223

八聲甘州　蘇軾　224

Bā-shēn gān-zhōu　Sū Shì　225

浣溪沙　周邦彥　226

Huān-xī shā　Zhōu Bāng-yàng　227

# 第五 英詩中譯
（Poems Translated from English into Chinese）

That Time of Year Thou May'st in Me Behold

　　—William Shakespeare　230

不久你將覺察我——威廉・莎士比亞　231

The Expense of Spirit—William Shakespeare　232

精力之消耗——威廉・莎士比亞　233

The Rape of the Lock—Alexander Pope　234

鬢髮遇劫記——亞歷山大・蒲柏　235

The Echoing Green—William Blake　236

回響草地——威廉・布萊克　237

"To See a World…"—William Blake　240

〈瞻世界…〉——威廉・布萊克　241

Ah, Sunflower—William Blake　240

啊，向日葵——威廉・布萊克　241

Composed upon Westminster Bridge—William Wordsworth　242

威斯敏斯特橋上所作——威廉・華茲華斯　243

I Wandered Lonely as a Cloud—William Wordsworth　244

獨自徜徉雲間——威廉・華茲華斯　245

In the Churchyard at Cambridge

　　—Henry Wadsworth Longfellow　248

劍橋的墓地裡——亨利・沃茲沃思・朗費羅　249

Inscription

For Mayre's Heights, Fredericksburg—Herman Melville　252

碑文

為弗雷德里克斯堡之瑪莉高地而作──赫爾曼‧梅爾維爾　253

Four Ducks on a Pond—William Allingham　252

塘上四鴨──威廉‧阿林漢姆　253

Memory—Thomas Bailey Aldrich　254

記憶──湯瑪斯‧貝雷‧阿爾曲奇　255

Somebody's Darling—Marie Ravenel de la Coste　256

人家的心上人──瑪麗‧拉維內爾德拉斯科斯特　257

Epitaph on an Army of Mercenaries—A.E. Houseman　262

雇傭軍的基誌銘──阿爾弗雷德‧愛德華‧豪斯曼　263

Easter—Geoffrey Anketell Studdert-Kennedy　264

復活節──傑佛瑞‧安克泰爾‧斯塔德特－甘迺迪　265

Dulce et Decorum Est—Wilfred Owen　266

以身殉國──維爾浮萊德‧歐文　267


附錄（Appendix）　270

# 輯一 雙語詩詞歌曲

（ Bilingual Poems and Lyrics ）

# 金婚吟

人生苦短歲華逸，老化痕跡此身密。
青春任憑不再來，一生相處飴如蜜。
五十寒冬共一堂，早晚家務纏身忙。
任勞任苦斷無怨，相夫教兒凡事當。
玉容豐滿已不恃，當鏡已覺鬢霜起。
滴滴辛勤千斛情，相共患難是知已。
如今慕儀恰如先，山盟海誓心猶堅。
一心所衷唯有妳，浩瀚蒼海千古緣。

# A Song of Golden Anniversary

This life, regrettably short as time fleets,
is so full of the effects of aging
that even if youth won't return again,
our life together is as sweet as honey.
Under the same roof, we have our life spent
together for fifty years. You've taken on house work
day and night, enduring its toil and moil
without complaints, as if taking on the whole
weight of caring for husband and children.
Your pulpy, jade-like complexion appears
haggard, and your hair turned gray, obvious
in the mirror. Behind each drop of your toil
there're thousand bushels of love. Through hardship
together, we become friends too close to be
apart. In the same way, I adore you now
as I did before and the deep-sworn vow
is as firm as afore. In my heart, you're
my only lover. This lasting fate grows
profuse like the main of ocean on Earth.

# 歡樂無比：給Fred及Leia

他們露天疊躺在
草地上，空氣清新
像發亮的薄冰片
他們雙雙微笑
彎著手臂
他的手臂放在頭後
她的放在頭上
二者身体各自挺直
像個特大的蜻蜓
臥伸在青草地上
悠閒自足
喜悅露在臉上
上帝的厚賜盡在不言中

——為Fred及Leia作於2017年

# Joys Beyond Words: To Fred and Leia

On a lawn, they lie piled
in open air, clear and fresh
like lucent ice-flakes,
both in gentle smiles.
They bend their arms,
one behind his head,
the other on top of her head,
and their bodies stretch at full length
like a giant dragonfly
spread-eagled on green grass,
at ease and content.
Their joys visible from their faces
are too much blessed by God to describe.

———Composed for Fred and Leia in 2017

# 寶寶

初夜的乳香
滯留在
你的搖籃裡
緣分就此
左右著
媽與你的命運
漫長的歲月
在哇哇聲中
敲響著
媽愛你的節奏
編織著
媽對你的期望

—— 為Alice及Alex作於2017年

# To My Babe

Since that first night,

when the scent of milk

still lingering in your cradle,

this mingling of fate perchance

has dictated our destiny –

mom's and yours –

and, in the long, drowned years

ahead of us, shall resonate,

amidst your loud cries, with the rhythm

of mom's love towards you,

weaving

mom's dream of your future.

——Composed for Alice and Alex in 2017

# 「妳」的正身

始於該頓的音調，必要男人作緊隨。
遵照英文的拼字，正身體貌顯呈誰。

# 詩人之專擅

詩人與哲人有異，
哲人倡《須定是謂》，
詩人典故當引喻，
常涉及理想主義，
玩弄神祕之想像，
藉此呈出其感受，
且用音色配合
節奏之巧妙韻律，
因其靈感之緣起在於登攀
而立足於《即如此》之信是，
以熱情期盼其讀者
之讚美為認可。

# The Selfie of "She"

It commences with a pause in its tone
and is accompanied closely by a man.
Through the spellings of alphabets
is the clue to the selfie of "she" disclosed.


# A Poet's License

Often risking idealism,
Whenever he composes a poem,
The poet, unlike a philosopher,
Who preaches "what should be,"
Presents his own experience
By manipulating the mystery
Of ideas through metaphorizing allusions
And conforms sonic colors with the cadence
Of a magic rhythm, for his inspiration
Climbs toward that perch where his belief
Of "what is" stands and he awaits with gusto
The approval of his admiring readers.

# 拾貝

晨霞才睜開惺忪眼
潮水已在說再見
留下魚鱗般的皺紋
在沙灘上排排展伸
千古失落海底的貝殼
終於脫身喜見人世
為了酬答早起的游客
傾倒出一簍簍海中的軼事

游人漫步沙上、低頭探望
好奇地彎身曲膝、頻頻
試著揀拾一則感人的奇聞

或許，好奇是天生的衝動
無中生有的盲從
希望與失望的煩惱
患得與患失的煎熬
是幻想與理智的交鋒

此刻，雲端深處，海風
正在見証一齣好奇的夢

# Shell-picking

As the flame of dawn has just opened her drowsy eyes,
The tide has already started to bid bye-bye,
Leaving curves on the beach, stretching
like fish scales in rows after rows.
Shells lost on the bottom of the sea since ancient times
Escape at last and are pleased to see the mundane world
And, to reward those travelers who rose in early morning,
Pouring out bundles of bundles of yarns of the sea.

Travelers stroll along the beach, their heads bowed, their eyes
looking around in curiosity, often with their bodies and knees bent,
trying to pick out a piece of an interesting anecdote.

Maybe, curiosity is of an impulse by nature,
A blind pursuit for something out of nothing,
An agony between hope and disappointment,
A torture of gauging losses over gains
And a confrontation between illusion and reasoning.

At the moment, far behind the clouds, the sea-wind
is witnessing an unfolding dream of curiosity.

# 賣樂肯[1]的從良婦

一片蒼苔海岸傍，賣樂肯濱有堤防。
平臥直伸嬌態顯，街燈依偎愛撫忙。
破曉遣使晨光聊，毅然厚顏熱情招。
蠢蠢欲動來滾浪，納她入懷激情撩。
娼婦從良綺夢求，芳心新愛仍未兜：
其愛滿如街燈溢，其語溫似晨曦柔。
彬彬有禮如鄰親，心胸豁達如海濱。

---

[1] 　賣樂肯是一條濱海大道的路名，在古巴首都哈瓦那。該處是一旅遊景點。

# Malecon's[1] Magdalene

A strip of blue-moss extends o'er the shore,
Where a seawall on Malecon's bank leans,
Lying stretched in coy pretense on display;
Street lights clinch to her in busy caress.
The breaking dawn sends his twilight to talk,
Shining up to her, brazen and direct.
The surging billow, edgy and eager,
Strains her to his bosom in thrilled embrace.
She, a magdalene, dreams a rosy dream
And for her fantasy finds no suitor:
Whose love be as outpouring as street lights,
Whose words be as pleasing as the twilight,
 Whose fair manner as friendly as neighbors,
Whose mind as open as the shores of the sea.

---

[1]  Malecon is the name of a boulevard along a seashore in Havana, Cuba. It is a tourist attraction.

# 晚年

斜陽淡淡餘暉辭，曖曖長空暮靄垂。
逝去青春無處覓，歡欣往事豈能追？
賞詩經日殊無厭，欲學詩人瀟灑喜。
偶得詩情分一角，可稱童境老來戲。

# 分秒必爭

在池旁，他們帶著急切的眼光，
像一條魚，潑濺出水——
又緊張、又害怕。
他們彼此爭先跳入自己的線內，
得採取一定的游姿：
雙手在胸前揮舞、
雙腳同時從二旁伸曲，
像青蛙，在窄線內起伏潛游，
僅幾分鐘就得見高下。

# Declining Years

The setting sun, pale and faded, departs with its light,
As the evening cloud dips into horizon o'er a gloomy sky.
While the vanished pride of youth won't return again,
Could the rejoices of bygone days ever be regained?
Delving in poetry in earnest all day long
Enlightens me to garner a poet's light-hearted soul
And the joy of a casual epiphany perceived
Vies with the recollection of childhood in declining years.


# Beating the Clock

By the pool, they met with keen eyes
ike a fish splashing out of the water –
as nervous, as afraid.
They dived past each other
into their own lanes with a style to test:
their hand-strokes must be in front of their chests,
and legs, in sync with hands, be stretched on sides.
Each heaving like a frog in a narrow lane,
they had only minutes to win the race.

# 邂逅

清脆潦亮
的簫簧
靠她靈活的手指
巧妙地
試出一曲新聲
他倆
眼神相勾
的秋波
橫慾相送
在懸崖下
相互擁抱
像蒼蠅纏在蛛絲中
頃刻
二人情意相投
感情昇華
卻於雲雨之後
感受索然麻木
他對她的狂戀
恰似
迷失於
春夢中

# An Encounter

With a bright sound
through the reed of a flute,
her nimble fingers,
flipping deftly,
tuned a new song.
A sly look
at each other's
bewitching eyes
in a flirting itch,
they tangled
under a cliff
like flies in cobwebs.
Before long,
they mingled together
and their feelings elevated,
yet turned dull
after the roll,
as though
his rave on her
was lost
in an erotic dream.

# 祝您生日快樂

一顆久經平靜的心
被生日的驚喜
不經意地
敲碎了心中的鏡子
掀起粼粼的水花
蕩漾著漣漪的祝福

# 今天

從朋友虔誠的祝福中
對滄桑的人生
有了新的體悟
真摯的友情
洋溢心中
那麼溫馨
那麼激昂
今天
這是一份難捨的壽禮

# Happy Birthday to You

A mind long posed in peace
is surprised in joy by the approaching
birthday that inadvertently
breaks its inner mirror into pieces,
stirring its surface with glittering ringlets
and dancing forth with ripples of blessings.

# Today

From the sincere blessings of friends,
there emerges a new insight
into the vicissitudes of life,
your heart is
brimmed with genuine friendship,
which, so warm and so passionate,
is a gift
that you won't part with
on this day of your birthday.

# 賀友人九十大壽

群花逐艷滿城春，喜氣洋洋慶壽辰。
開始人生僅九十，得天獨厚康強身。
休言孟子瞠乎後，笑讓孔丘步後塵。
蕭灑一生風騷領，傲睨老子百歲真。

# 赤子心

噢，不必偽飾
要像緊抱著舊書的讀書人一樣
與自古受尊的賢人為伍──
他們的睿智閃爍在褪色的紙上──
不羨他人之盛名
安於一已謙虛的心靈
在慎重的一刻恆求良言
不摻激動及罪惡

# In Celebration of a Friend's Ninetieth Birthday

The splurges of flowers spread the springtime to the whole city;
We all come in a jaunty mood to celebrate your birthday.
To you, life has just begun at the age of ninety
And our Lord's unique blessing is your never-ending life.
Let's keep quiet that Mencius pales in comparison with your age
And in your footsteps you, in smile, let Confucius follow.
A pioneer in longevity throughout your lofty life,
You dare to beat Laozi's age of one hundred years old.


# A Naked Mind

O to pretend not, like a bookman
staying tethered to tattered books,
making friends with time-honored sages –
their wisdom sparkling on faded pages –
envious of no great fame but content
with a humble soul of a solemn
moment that forever seeks advice.
unpolluted with impulse and vice.

# 墓地之前廳

冥間離此呎尺邊，同伴此居皆暫遷。
渴望安寧好去處，一生在此過餘年。
每當兒女傍持孝，職工悉呈職業貌。
看似照護有溫情，溫吞語氣誠意稍。
有意無心之愛衷，笑容僵化強裝充。
一旦兒女不來訪，假貌畢露殷勤終。
授受不當自尊失，待我當成為木質。
儘是佯裝來正經，我雖作息但無逸。
試圖分明其懶惰，不顧同情兼欠誠。
欠顧不應謂照護，服侍生成苛待生。
生活難逃懈怠棄，沾污專業之屬類。
無情大廳之職工，不意驅人到墓地。

# A Hall to Graveyard

Here, one step from hades,
Reside short-term companions,
All seeking a peaceful place
For the last stretch of their journey to depart.
When my daughter is with me,
The staff show a professional face,
Their caring lukewarm with a tone tepid,
Their loving half-hearted with a smile stereotyped.
Changed no sooner but revealed their real face
During the time when I miss her –
Indecent touch,
Indifferent to my self-respect,
Treating me like an inanimate object –
All working in pretension.
I try to bring in some sense to their neglect:
Caring is not caring that belies
Sympathy, when it fills with apathy.
My caregivers are my torturers,
Their sly inattentiveness overshadows my livelihood.
Such shame tarnishes their professional characters.
Here, an insensible hall, its staff
Unwittingly goading me to a graveyard.

# 孤雁[1]

楓葉滿山紛起落，嶺上晚風淒。夕陽樹外，四方寥寂，孤雁掠空啼。
南歸萬里顛危冒，頂著勁風齊。每逢落泊，慘愁暗箭，何處得投棲。

---

[1] 做少年游而填。

# A Lone Goose[1]

In the air, maple leaves swirled up and down
all over the mountain, as the frigid
wind blew o'er its peak in the evening.
Beyond the forest the sun was setting
down, while all the surroundings in sight were
in sheer desolation. A lone goose cried
scudding over the sky for a journey
to the South, which was treacherous and miles
of miles away, often with gusts of wind
to face and with grave concerns about
the traps of sneaky snipers to tackle,
unsure of a safe place to settle down,
whenever making an attempt to perch.

---

[1]    To the tune Shǎo-nián yóu.

# 懷念

叢林瑟瑟雪飄吹，入室寒光月竊窺。
去歲此時傷別後，天人永隔寄相思。

# 闊別

杜鵑枝上弄啁啾，艷紅楓葉又當秋。
去國相別有三載，杳無音訊更生憂。

# Reminiscence

In the rustling forest snow swirls.
Through the cold light casting inside the moon peeks.
Your heart-broken death, a year ago to this day, puts me
In mind of you as far apart as heaven and earth.

# A Long Hiatus

Cuckoos are busy chirping on branches;
Maple leaves' colors are dazzling and rich.
You have departed the land for three good years
With no news at all, worsening my grieves.

# 賞鬱金香

鬱金香圖翠，中有一天使，
身著紅冬衣，行人表讚意。
鬱金香亦羨。沉靜安詳面，
優雅臉容顯，眼笑迷人現。
凝視溫柔深，頓開鬱結心，
如日慰絕望。設如憂愁臨。
每逢臉龐窺，堪慰創傷治。

——作於Leia生日，2014年11月30日

# Adoring Tulips

Behind the mosaic of tulips,

There an angel stands.

A red Eskimo coat she wears,

Which the passersby adore

And the tulips do envy.

Her graceful face a serene look discloses.

Charming as her eyes, and as tender as her stares,

She brightens the dark soul

And, like the sun, warms the despair.

If, by chance, sorrows do ever fall,

Look on her face, all the wounds would be soothed.

——Composed on Leia's birthday, November 30, 2014

# 一事無成

恨命不如嶺上鶯，東西南北任翱翔。
空酬壯志年華逝，落葉歸根更待行。

# Nothing Accomplished

I envy that eagle over the mountain cliff,

Capable of flying to everywhere at ease,

While none of my noble deeds are done, as time fleets,

Even including that often sought home-bound trip!

# 輯一 中文詩詞
（Poems and Lyrics Composed in Chinese）

# 媽的諾言

一個海外遊子
在阡陌青蔥的田野上
摸索著秧苗與記憶的距離
尋找母親的葬地

媽病危的期間
正是那兵倒如山的時代
那時，不論男女老幼
即使溪山隱遁
即使雲月無爭
都聽不由己
各奔東西
媽的棺木
草率的埋在田畦旁

我隨家遷居台灣
過著失去母愛的童年
孩提時，常常夢見媽
幫我穿衣上學
低著頭、彎著身
粗糙的雙手
捧著我的面頰
微笑的臉容
關懷的眼神
耐心地、再三叮嚀
像生前那般慈祥

# 媽的諾言（續）

媽一病不起
滿身水泡
不明的病情
早晚為她挑泡去癢
不只一次答應我說：
「待媽病好後、給乖乖做桂花糕吃」

時光遞遞、兩地迢迢
媽在丘塚上
無奈的等著
那半甲子的時光

我走到田埂上
輕喚著：「媽……」
彷彿墓塚裡的岑寂
像千古封存的記憶
徐徐甦醒、悄悄的
慰撫著我對媽永世的懷念

我、獨思媽媽的允諾
童年未曾兌現
晚年已是圓缺
從小時到現在
是美夢也是碎夢

# 秋色繽紛

扶桑初出、人聲零落
林中已有薄薄涼意

伴著晨色漫步林間
溪旁魚水輕語
晨光落落篩下
喚醒樹上的松鼠
輕撩蓬鬆的尾巴
向我噗哧地一笑

不知何時、輕風漸生
周遭楓葉窸窣
身後迂迴小徑
隨著水聲的流淌
漸漸隱入
豔紅淡黃的一片樹海

秋意漸濃
挾著色彩
到處潑墨猶自未了

# 安養院263室的病人

意識與脊椎
結盟的地方
絲絲血絲中
一叢叢
小小的細胞
頑固地不再翻騰

我想舒伸手足
左右挪動身子
卻拗不過麻木的四肢
我真羨慕那蜘蛛
任性的躡足軟步
在染塵的窗格上
寫下神奇的蝌蚪文
嫉妒讓我激起一陣陣
聲聲的感嘆

唉、無聲無望的矛盾
鼓蕩著癱瘓的淒楚
空蕩蕩的頭殼
罩不住無奈的折磨
靠眼珠的蠕動
思忖著四肢的頑強
只因惛懵的大腦
沉滯於混沌的時光中

# 庵寺怨

荒度流年潘鬢顯，紅塵往事思猶泫。
昨夜雪飄低暗落，松柏窗後冷相展。
寺院蕭瑟新月形，宮內嫦娥空守庭。
猶憶當年月下誓，真情互融溫又馨。
橫刀奪愛愛相悖，因變而變愛非愛。
山盟海誓狠心破，青春從此駐庵內。
皈依菩薩慧根純，清心寡慾超世塵。
廟前雲月海光照，歲月無憑復無循。
潮來潮去痛心淚，那堪回首舊情棄。
此世永訣斷不見，來世相逅定垂涕。

# 祝壽有感

難逢千載好機緣，四位壽星來入筵。
無法遷移歲月逝，恰逢喜日情翩翩。
處處嫣紅楓葉蹤，天河冷落秋意濃。
席中笑語又歌起，喜氣洋溢忘龍鍾。
青春已逝如蠶蛾，老邁戰兢迎百痾。
雄抱難展一生憾，力不從心歎奈何！
羈居北國怎捨還，猶夢來時蹤迹艱。
但願恆久常相聚，相互關懷迎晚年。

# 憶亡夫

春花秋雨兼數冬，怎奈永離隔九重。
曉星寥落晨光淡，寒衾輾轉誰與同。
萬象蕭瑟冬雪飛，春風群花索寞揮。
音容神色仍縈繞，無垠雲羅夢依稀。
猶憶昔日結縭喜，心心相許終生陪。
那年驚悉臨終語，鴛鴦淒愴春心衰。
從此影形單隻多，淚如縻絚無奈何。
孤苦無告伶仃嘆，晼晚此生何以過。


# 友人八十大壽有感

生活像顏料
在油布上留下
動人的畫面
八十年的生活
像一位多才多藝的畫家
在人生舞臺上著墨
刻意地展現生命的真諦
留下無數美麗又珍貴的回憶

# 更漏子

點滴流，輪椅坐，癱瘓淒淒身裏。眼呆滯，腦茫茫，病因入膏肓。
吾妻嫋，賢慧嬌，吾欲老相少愀。體羸弱，下身痿，夢圓難以期。

# 長生嘆

嫦娥雖有萬靈藥，夜夜難挨少女心。
不老長生千古夢，強身鍛鍊健康臨。

# 太平島塔燈修竣有感

先民遺址今猶在，千里光芒主權存。
磐石萬年成砥柱，南疆屹立中華魂。

# 故宅

驟雨斜風陣陣吹，祖居淒寂頹然危。
童年綺麗依稀夢，晚晚人生空自悲。


# 遊黃山有感

錦繡黃山入雲霧，濛濛幻境飄捲迎。
相離半世仍羞怯，落葉歸根未了情。


# 安養院的老人

蒼穹向晚寥，白雪滿庭飄。
漫漫恰如絮，茫茫生死熬。

# 遊織金洞有感

怪異靈奇織金洞，溶岩矗立億年融。
光怪陸離萬千象、墨客騷人盡筆窮。

# 黯鄉魂[1]

憑欄佇立空歎欷，滿陵冬色寒松翠。落寞深怨私自愧，飄雪墜，恰如遊子潸潸淚。
愧對神州憂祖地，迢迢千里丹心熾。雲月渺茫鄉魂碎，夜深至，殘燈孤影人難寐。

---

[1] 倣漁家傲而填。1989年訪河北大學返加後作。

# 灑脫

奸邪論斷恁誰尊？世態炎涼不落煩。
豁達真誠應本性，人生坎坷喜來吞。

# 人性[1]

人性無形恆欠常，好心壞意莫名呈，務惡伴善少真誠。
方寸把持之反照，心情外表難分明，包羅人世眾生相。

# 菩薩蠻

南柯一夢人生短、衷腸往事幽幽展。昔日許奴身、山誓海盟珍。
絕情私自棄，不解為何背。感慨萬千情，老來仍恨輕。

---

[1] 倣浣溪沙而填。

# 晨起獨白

白雪溚溚拂山谷，徐徐曙色漸現晨。
淺眠覺醒漫長夜，空嘆朦朧瘦弱身。
一寸光陰一寸逝，千愁萬慮憂心頻。
年華急逼誠難擋，恨命辛勞志不伸。

# 老來嘆

人生似流星，倏忽成幻形。
青絲化白髮，年歲已高齡。
友情誠可愛，相惜愈形惺。
富貴已無就，青雲飄逸靈。

# 輯二 英詩

（ Poems Composed in English ）

# To My Other Father

Your fatherly love, among other things,
in my heart endures; not only the benevolence
of yours in brining me up will be remembered,
but your belief in me and patience
shown throughout my adolescence.
What I have learned from you in person
is to do what I believe is right
and to pursue the value of a simple life:
transient in this world are wealth and titles,
while loving and caring in heart truly lasting.
You are but of an ordinary citizen,
yet, an exemplar of a great uncle!
Composed in memory of your death on July 19th, 1994.

# To Our Dearest Leia

On this first birthday of yours,
Joy to the family roars:
The true meaning of life heightened,
And hope for the future brightened.
Your smiles are like red roses,
Your sweet eyes like shining dews.
Since your birth the pace of your growth
Enriches the rhythm of our love.
(From Grandpa, Grandma, and Uncle Nick
November 30, 2013, at 11:00 a.m.)

# To Larry and Melissa

While in mathematics,

two is made of one plus one,

in marriage,

one plus one merges into a true One.[1]

Not a science

is marriage,

which, in essence,

is a matter of affection –

a kind of love, sincere and romantic,

that, like a plan to invest,

demands to be nurtured,

little by little,

through constant devotion

before reaping its harvest.

---

[1] Genesis 2:23.

# In Memory of the God-Man

In Gethsemane, nearby the Golgotha,
Where His "god-ness" and "man-ness" both pierced,
Each by devil's craft forever tortured.
The Son of Man bowed; the Son of God triumphed.
Divinity and humanity adjoined,
Forcing the devil to exit.
Peace and love conjoined;
Humans and all creatures coexist.


# Why I Want to Know Him More?

The longing for knowing Him better,
The release from darkness to light,
from an obstinate ignorance, forgiven
by the grace of His blessing, tender
and enlightening, both the good and the evil
blinded by ignorance alike made explicit,
guiding the choice of right and wrong
along the journey of my spiritual life.

# Grasp Without Reach?

A touch of inspiration in a moment
of reflection, I sharpen the knives
of my wisdom and seek the vision of God
to lead me to a life of rectitude
like a seminarian.

And somewhere deep in my soul
are the hungry eyes searching
for the standards of God
like a beggar.

I do not stop to grasp God's meaning
but I have never reached. Should
my grasp exceed my reach
without jeopardizing my standing
in the presence of God's grace?

# Atonement

I am what I was – soul,
I was not what I am – body,
Once sanctified, I am both:
Life ever-lasting.


# The Sound of Silence in a Nursing Home

A fit of impulse in a wintry morning,
I walked to Pine Ridge
and saw residents lean against
tables like playing porker.
Far around a corner was Ray,
his head drooped as if in deep thought.
Buried in a cold wheel-chair
and having owned it for so long, now
he couldn't recognize his visitors.
Silence permeated among his despairs
like in a memorial service
and he could hear its hushed steps
around him, as if drowning
in the sound of silence – death.

# Second to None?

See how the Earth its paradox belies!
The finite juxtaposes with the infinite,
the known with the unknown,
the oneness with the none-ness,
along with its claim of the only Mind
amidst the swelling millions
that performs its theatrics
on the stage of galaxies.

# The Innocent

Hear, hear, there, you parrot!
You are so ignorant,
As mere sounds are your words.
Your tongue is truly cute,
Because it's not as rude
As your cunny master.

# Class Reunion

See how they cherish their class reunion:
Eager in wistful appearance, warm in pure passion,
Memories of good time, elders in frolics,
Sparkling eyes in high glee, teasing puns to no end,
A reunion of dreams, a surprise their prize,
Active and agile, gay and great!

# The True Color of Lies

A liar's lies are like rumors that haunt us
like swirling snowflakes, their gist all based
on fabrications and their motive aimed
at distortion of facts like a depraved
soul rooted in a decadent body
or a heart drown in a vicious conceit
all coming from a sinful mind, as much
muddled as the cabin of a sunk ship
in which darkness extends beyond darkness.

# Politicians' Gimmick

We relish politicians' wish
to seek support from the public,
who are elated by their rhetoric
serving as a decoy to coax voters,
their deceit well-conceived,
though their greed for power
falls in disgrace with the electorate:
first, hypnotized, then disillusioned,
and, at last, disenchanted
by politicians' cynicism.

# Doctor-assisted Death

Alone in a wheelchair, as if waiting
for an end, a patient in a nursing
home, she droops her head deep in thought, her mind
gripped in the vicious vise of fear and blows –
the fear of losing a quality life, blows
to self-esteem that no words could describe –
her body in writhing struggle to vanish.
She, in the main of sorrow and grief, wishes
to summon the time and date of her death.
By so much the better, she is determined to
throw the omniscient God into neglect.


# A Living Stone Without a Soul

This, a place of shadows with dark corners
to hell where a living stone without a soul
awaits a last dash to complete its dim dot
for real, is a plot without acquaintance
that becomes impatient about its owner
drown in a sinful life without repentance.

# The Man Who Spoils His Boss at Home

Never he is moody
and he rarely argues,
always spending his evenings
in the kitchen, cutting meats and veggies
in the right size and shape, as told.
He does laundry on Saturdays,
sorting clothes by colors and categories
dictated by his chief, as if showing
an account book in exact details
with credits and debits, never misplaced.
Lowliness makes him feel shamefaced:
each occurrence of an obedient mood
audible from his tone,
furtive like a cat
and nervous like a rat.
Whenever she reacts, he is in agony,
his humors stuttering
in front of a chief
too serious to tease.

# The Specter of Death

Swirling outside in the dark,
the wind breaks through the window,
forcing crackled candle-lights to draw graffiti
on the wall like a drunk artist.
The wind shakes the calendar,
innocent and agitated,
and flips through marked
dates of doctor appointments
in the air: an aging body, living
the last stretch to heaven –
a simple reality facing complex sufferings –
with a touch of sadness he soon has to swallow.

# Crib Death

He lies on his tummy
like a cute baby seal
his stiff face buried deep
in a snow-white bedsheet,
arms along with body
covered by a blanket.
What an odd tragedy
to regret in surprise –
to remember for life.

# The Irony of Excitement

An odd mark printed on my forehead,
clung to a wandering mind,
yearning blindly for winning big,
I sobbed whenever the winning ticket
slipped away, killing as much the excitement
as I had hoped, though I often fancied myself to ride
on the wings of prayer for God's blessings.
Here I am – with a hopeful chance to win
likely slim, still keep buying,
holding a new ticket in hand,
child-like mouth wide open,
ready for a renewed excitement!

# A Short Visit

We stood by the convent that windy evening
and the waves were receding,
as if the moaning of anger,
my hands hesitant to reach yours
that were so familiar before.
Your stares were as stares that search
for riddles unanswered for years
and for memories long lost due to our divorce.
Your insecurity shown on your face before
was the most obvious mark visible
enough to explain your departure.
Since then, sad lesson love taught you,
and with a faith in God, has given you
a life, now submitted to the way of living
dictated by your Mother Superior.

中詩（英）譯輯

（Poems and Lyrics Translated from Chinese into English）

# 詩經・周南・桃夭

桃之夭夭，灼灼其華。之子於歸，宜其室家。
桃之夭夭，有蕡其實。之子於歸，宜其家室。
桃之夭夭，其葉蓁蓁。之子於歸，宜其家人。

# The Book of Songs · Odes of Zhou and South · The Tào-yāo

Like a peach tree in sturdy growth
With flowers blushing and dazzling,
She's a mate ready to tie the knot
And is ideal to be a spouse.
Like a peach tree in luxuriant growth
With peaches corpulent and dangling,
She's a mate ready to tie the knot
And is ideal to form a family now.
Like a peach tree in vigorous growth
With leaves thick and flourishing,
She's a mate ready to tie the knot
And is ideal to have her in the house.

# 飲酒（第七首） 陶淵明

秋菊有佳色，裛露掇其英。
泛此忘憂物，遠我遺世情。
一觴雖獨盡，杯盡壺自傾。
日入群動息，歸鳥趨林鳴。
嘯傲東軒下，聊複得此生。

# Drinking Wine (No. 7)
# Táo Yuān-ming

Dazzling in fall are Chrysanthemums
And I pluck their flowers wet with dews.
Flushed with this worry-free stuff
That keeps me away from this domain
Of mortal world, I get slushed alone
And buzz the wine-jar cup after cup.
By sunset when creatures starting to roost
And returning birds chattering in woods,
I live a cloistered life by an east window,
Trying to get life back on track again.

# 飲酒（第十三首）　陶淵明

有客常同止，取捨邈異境。
一士長獨醉，一夫終年醒。
醒醉還相笑，發言各不領。
規規一何愚，兀傲差若穎。
寄言酣中客，日沒燭當秉。

# Drinking Wine (No. 13)
# Táo Yuān-ming

Two quests often come across together,
Whose outlooks do radically differ:
One, a scholar, is often drunk alone;
One, a commoner, sober all year long.
The rapt and the sober mock at each other,
Their words doom to reach a meeting of minds.
One, rigid in thought, is a lowbrow rather;
One, smug and cocky, is somewhat wiser.
To those fond of wine, accept my advice
To keep drinking by a lit candle all night.

# 敦煌曲子詞集・傾杯樂

憶昔笄年，未省離合，生長深閨院。閒凭著繡床，時拈金針，擬貌舞鳳飛鸞。對妝臺重整嬉恣面。自身後算料，豈教人見。又被良媒，苦出言詞相誘炫。

每道說水際鴛鴦，惟指梁間雙燕。被父母將兒匹配，便認多生宿姻眷。一旦娉得狂夫，攻書業，拋妾求名宦。縱然選得，一時朝要，榮華爭穩便。

# Dunhuang Quziciji · Ch'ing-pei lo

I remember when I attained adolescence,

I was unaware of the meaning of separation and reunion.

Growing up in an inner chamber,

I leaned on an embroidered bed in my vacant hours,

Often trying, with a golden needle,

To quilt the images of dancing and flying phoenixes.

I applied make-up to my best before a dressing table,

Indulging myself in self-appreciation

With no intent for others to admire me.

And then a clever matchmaker's

Sweet-talk deluded me.

People often said mandarin ducks live by water,

Though I believe they meant paired swallows live amidst girders.

When my parents arranged a marriage for me,

I submitted myself entirely to my partner,

Unaware that once the crazy fool and I became one flesh,

He would care more about books than me in seeking an official career.

I wonder even if he has gained a high official title

And become an important courtier,

How long he could keep his honor and glory?

# 鹿柴　王維

空山不見人，但聞人語響。
返影入深林，複照青苔上。

# 哥舒歌　西鄙人

北斗七星高，哥舒夜帶刀。
至今窺牧馬，不敢過臨洮。

# Lù Chái　Wang Wei

O'er the dead mount, no men are visible,
Though their hurly-burly is audible.
The reflected light peers through the dense woods,
And never stops coating the green mosses.

# A Song in Honor of General Gēshū
# Author Unknown

While the Plough's seven stars were high in the sky,
General Gēshū was in full arms at night,
Holding the frontier Tartars at bay till now,
Who dared not to cross the outskirt of Lintao.

# 越中覽古　李白

越王勾踐破吳歸，義士還家盡錦衣。
宮女如花滿春殿，只今惟有鷓鴣飛。

# 菩薩蠻　李白

平林漠漠煙如織，寒山一帶傷心碧。暝色入高樓，有人樓上愁。
玉階空佇立，宿鳥歸飛急。何處是歸程？長亭更短亭。

## Touring the Relics in the Middle Land of the Yuè    Li Po

When the King of Yuè was back from crushing the King of Wú,
His chivalrous warriors returned, all in finest array,
And his elated palace full of fair court-ladies.
Now, nothing has left but partridges flying by ruins.

## Pú-sà mán    Li Po

Mists, as thick as knitted, shroud the forest
And the greenery appears pathetic along the chilly mountain.
As the hue of night into the tall tower creeps,
Someone is in sorrow upstairs.

I stand waiting in vain on jaded stairs,
While home-bound birds hurry to their nests.
To where should this return trip lead me
Through one posthouse after another at varied distances?

# 月下獨酌　李白

花間一壺酒，獨酌無相親。
舉杯邀明月，對影成三人。
月既不解飲，影徒隨我身。
暫伴月將影，行樂須及春。
我歌月徘徊，我舞影凌亂。
醒時同交歡，醉後各分散。
永結無情遊，相期邈雲漢。

# Drinking Alone in Moonlight　Li Po

Amidst flowers where a pot of wine I hold,

Drinking alone with no friends around,

I raise my cup to invite the bright moon to come,

Forming a group of three including my shadow.

The moon, wine-drinking to learn,

And the shadow, tagging along behind my back,

 We, single as a triplet, befriend for now with each other

And must cut loose before spring is over.

Singing with the moon hanging around

And dancing with shadows as scattered as tangled,

We are all upbeat together, while awake,

And vanished after a dead drunk.

Let's gain a friendship growing with no end

Until we meet again on the milky way.

月下獨酌　李白／099

# 春日醉起言志　李白

處世若大夢，胡為勞其生。
所以終日醉，頹然臥前楹。
覺來眄庭前，一鳥花間鳴。
借問此何時，春風語流鶯。
感之欲歎息，對酒還自傾。
浩歌待明月，曲盡已忘情。

# Life Perceived After Waking up from a Drink in Springtime　Li Po

Living in this world is like a big dream.

Why torture yourself to make a living?

That is why I get dead drunk all the day.

By the front pillar I lie dejected,

Leering at the front court when I awake,

While amidst flowers a bird is chattering.

Pardon me, bird, what season is this, tell me?

"The Vernal breeze chats with a singing oriole,"

Is the reply, which makes me to lament,

And with wine, I still keep serving myself.

I troll a song for the moon to appear

And forget my feelings as my notes have ended.

# 春日憶李白　杜甫

白也詩無敵，飄然思不群。
清新庾開府，俊逸鮑參軍。
渭北春天樹，江東日暮雲。
何時一樽酒，重與細論文。

# 畫鷹　杜甫

素練風霜起，蒼鷹畫作殊。
聳身思狡兔，側目似愁胡。
絛鏇光堪摘，軒楹勢可呼。
何當擊凡鳥，毛血灑平蕪。

# Thinking of Li Po on a Spring Day
# Dù Fǔ

Li Po's poetry has of course no parallels,
His creativeness far exceeds his equals.
His style is as lucid and fresh as Minister Yǔ's
And his manner is as aloof as Counsellor Bào's.
In north of River Wei, there are trees in springtime,
In east of Yangtze, there are clouds of dusk.
When could we share another jug of wine
And meet again the details of poetics to discuss?

# A Painted Hawk　Dù Fǔ

On a white silk-cloth, the wind and the frost
Appear stirred up in a unique drawing
Of a painted hawk that into the sky soars,
Wishing to snatch cunning hares, its oblique glance
Resonant of a worried Hun's look. its chain and ring
Almost unchecked. Hung in the porch, the painted hawk
Is about to dash out, as if launching attacks
Against common birds, with their feathers
And blood splashed over the wild pasture.

# 怨詩　孟郊

試妾與君淚，兩處滴池水。
看取芙蓉花，今年為誰死。

# 問劉十九　劉禹錫

綠蟻新醅酒，紅泥小火爐。
晚來天欲雪，能飲一杯無？

# A Poem of Despair    Mèng Jiāo

Let us, you and me, try to cry afar
With tears pouring into ponds at two spots
And see for which of us the lotus flowers
Would be drowned and died this year first.


# An Invitation to Liú Shijiǔ    Liú Yǔ-xī

The foaming wine has just unstrained become,
And is heated on a little red-clay stove.
When night draws dawn, soon about to fall is snow,
I'll stand you to a drink, if you care to come.

# 浪濤沙　劉禹錫

八月濤聲吼地來，頭高數丈觸山回。
須臾卻入海門去，捲起沙堆似雪堆。

# 戲贈友人　賈島

一日不作詩，心源如廢井。
筆硯為轆轤，吟詠作縻綆。
朝來重汲引，依舊得清冷。
書贈同懷人，詞中多苦辛。

# Làng-tāo shà    Liú Yǔ-xī

In the month of August roll in the wave's roars,
Heaping their crests high in the air against the rocks,
Their surges receding in a blink from the shore
To the Sea-Gate, hurling sand dunes that pile like snow.

# To a Friend for Fun    Jiǎ Dǎo

A day spent without composing a poem
Makes inspiration like a ruined well.
The brush and the ink-slab are my tackle
And reciting poems is my hoisting rope.
The next morning's attempt to draw and pull
Still gets refreshing water from the well.
A composed poem sent to like-minded folks
Often contains words of arduous efforts.

浪濤沙　劉禹錫／戲贈友人　賈島／107

# 送人東遊　溫庭筠

荒戌落黃葉，浩然離故關。
高風漢陽渡，初日郢門山。
江上幾人在，天涯孤棹還。
何當重相見，樽酒慰離顏。

# Seeing a Friend off to the East
# Wēn Ting-jūn

As yellow leaves falling in a ruined fortress,
You were determined to leave the old pass.
On the high wind at the Hànyáng Ferry
You did reach Mount Yǐngmén by sunrise.
Few friends were along the riverside,
Afar, your lonely boat was sailing for home.
When should we gather again to have
A toast and to sooth the parting sorrow?

# 更漏子（一）　溫庭筠

柳絲長，春雨細，花外漏聲迢遞。驚塞雁，起城烏，畫屏金鷓鴣。
香霧薄，透簾幕，惆悵謝家池閣。紅燭背，繡簾垂，夢長君不知。

# Gèng-lòu zì (No. 1)　　Wēn Ting-jūn

Long as willow twigs
And soft as vernal rain,
Ticks a clepsydra beyond flowers afar,
Its distant clicking startles wild geese from the North
And stirs crows from their rest on the city wall,
As if the unease of golden partridges displayed
On a partition. Amidst thin and fragrant mists
Piercing through window draperies,
I pine for you by Xiè's pavilion and pond.
The red candle-light now guttered out
And embroidered curtains weighed down,
Can't you tell how long my dream is?

# 更漏子（二）　溫庭筠

背江樓，臨海月，城上角聲嗚咽。堤柳動，島煙昏，兩行征雁分。
京口路，歸帆渡，正是芳菲欲度。銀燭盡，玉繩低，一聲村落雞。

# Gèng-lòu zì (No. 2)　Wēn Ting-jūn

In front of a tower by the water,

The rising moon across the sea kindles

And from the top of city wall a bugle moans.

With sallow on the riverbank swinging

And the islet coated by smog in evening,

Returning geese are flying apart in arrays.

Leading to the Town of Jīngkǒu is a quay

Where a home-bound boat has moored,

As spring blossoms are withering.

When the silver candle light consumed

And the Jade Rope slanting low,

The cocks in nearby villages start to crow.

# 更漏子（三）　溫庭筠

金雀釵，紅粉面，花裡暫時相見。知我意，感君憐，此情須問天。
香作穗，蠟成淚，還似兩人心意。山枕膩，錦衾寒，覺來更漏殘。

# Gèng-lòu zì (No. 3)　Wēn Ting-jūn

Wearing a golden-sparrow hairpin

With a face, white and blushing,

I met you amidst flowers only for a while.

You knew what did I mean

And your compassion I did feel:

The Lord ought to attest our love.

Though into ashes the incense burnt

And into tears candle light turned,

Feelings were much the same between us.

As tears dropped on my pillows all night

And the embroidered quilt turned cold,

The clepsydra had almost drained when I awoke.

# 更漏子（四）　溫庭筠

玉爐香，紅蠟淚，偏照畫堂秋思。眉翠薄，鬢雲殘，夜長衾枕寒。梧桐樹，三更雨，不道離情正苦。一葉葉，一聲聲，空階滴到明。

# Gèng-lòu zì (No. 4)　Wēn Ting-jūn

With the scent of a jade censer in the air flowing
And the tears of a red candle still dropping,
A painted hall was permeated with grief in fall.
Brushed with green make-up, the eye-brows
Were in a lighter tint and the bouncy
Hair was tangled in a mess – a night, long enough to make
Pillow and quilt turn cold. Through phoenix trees,
The rain spattered after the wee hours, as if ignoring
The pain of bidding adieu. Leaves, piece by piece,
Rustled one after another, as the rain
Kept dropping on deserted steps till dawn.

# 菩薩蠻（一）　溫庭筠

玉樓明月長相憶，柳絲嬝娜春無力。門外草萋萋，送君聞馬嘶。
畫羅金翡翠，香燭銷成淚。花落子規啼，綠窗殘夢迷。

# 菩薩蠻（二）　溫庭筠

小山重疊金明滅，鬢雲欲度香腮雪。懶起畫蛾眉，弄妝梳洗遲。
照花前後鏡，花面交相映。新帖繡羅襦，雙雙金鷓鴣。

# Pú-sà mán (No. 1)　Wēn Ting-jūn

The moon was bright and in a jade tower
I often pined for you. As tender as slender,
The willow twigs were dangling in listless spring
And the grass overgrown outside. When seeing
You depart, I could hear the horse neigh.
By a gauze curtain painted with a red-feathered finch,
Fragrant candles were consumed in tears. Trilling
Amidst falling flowers were cuckoos. By a green
Window, I woke up in despair from a waking dream.

# Pú-sà mán (No. 2)　Wēn Ting-jūn

Painted in gold on a screen are layered hillocks,
Now half-faded and half-brown. With bouncy hair
across her cheeks, scented and in snow-white,
She is slow to knit her crescent-shaped eyebrows,
Leaving make-up and fresh-up behind.
Viewing flowers in a mirror with a one behind,
She notices her face vying for mirror images,
While changing to a new silk-wear
Embroidered with a pair of golden partridges.

# 商山早行　溫庭筠

晨起動征鐸，客行悲故鄉。
雞聲茅店月，人迹板橋霜。
槲葉落山路，枳花明驛牆。
因思杜陵夢，鳧雁滿迴塘。

# 無題　李商隱

相見時難別亦難，東風無力百花殘。
春蠶到死絲方盡，蠟炬成灰淚始乾。
曉鏡但愁雲鬢改，夜吟應覺月光寒。
蓬山此去無多路，青鳥殷勤為探看。

# Morning Departure from Mountain Shāng  Wēn Ting-jūn

I rose at dawn to mount a bell to my horse-cart,
A bitter nostalgia filled my mind on the road.
While cocks crowing in moonlight o'er a thatched store,
The frost of a wooden bridge bore tracks of footprints.
Mountain paths were dappled with leaves of Daimyo oaks;
Citron flowers kindled the walls of a post house.
All that led me to recall my dreams of Tu Ling,
Where ducks and geese paddling round and round on a pond.

# Untitled  Lǐ Shāng-yǐn

My feeling of leaving you is as difficult as seeing you,
Hurting me like flowers withered by the dying eastern wind,
Much like spring silkworms releasing threads till death
And a candle dripping its tears until burned into ashes.
At dawn, I fear my bouncy hair getting sparse before a mirror
And at night when reciting poems I feel cold under the moonlight.
There are no roads to the Fairy Mountain Péng where you live
And I shall send my sincere blessings to you by a blue bird.

商山早行　溫庭筠／無題　李商隱／121

# 寄令狐郎中　李商隱

崇雲秦樹久離居，雙鯉迢迢一紙書。
休問梁園舊賓客，茂陵秋雨病象如。

# 落花　李商隱

高閣客竟去，小園花亂飛。
參差連曲陌，迢遞送斜暉。
腸斷未忍掃，眼穿仍欲稀。
芳心向春盡，所得是沾衣。

# A Message to Official Līng Hú
## Lǐ Shāng-yǐn

For ages, under the clouds of Chóng
And trees of Qín, we have been living apart.
A letter has reached me far away
From here by chance. Please, don't ask the old
Guest at the Liang Garden, who, like Xiāng Rú,
Is sick at Mào Líng in autumn rain.


# Falling Flowers    Lǐ Shāng-yǐn

From a high pavilion, guests are vying to leave,
Flowers of a small garden gyrate to the wind,
Their messy petals scatter along winding roads,
Bidding farewell far away to the sun parting,
And I cannot bear to sweep them away in grief,
Keen to see the pause of their insistent wilting.
Their fragrant hearts strain hard to feast my eyes in spring,
Before their petals wind up dropping on my robe.

# 嫦娥　李商隱

雲母屏風燭影深，長河漸落曉星沉。
嫦娥應悔偷靈藥，碧海青天夜夜心。

# 無題（一）　李商隱

鳳尾香羅薄幾重，碧文圓頂夜深縫。
扇裁月魄羞難掩，車走雷聲語未通。
曾是寂寥金燼暗，斷無消息石榴紅。
斑騅只系垂楊岸，何處西南任好風。

# The Moon Goddess　Lǐ Shāng-yǐn

The dark shadow of a candle light
Is on a mica screen. As the milky way
Is setting, the stars have already declined.
The Moon Goddess should regret to take
The elixir of life, facing the blue sea
and sky – a lonely heart bereft every night feels.

# Untitled (No. 1)　Lǐ Shāng-yǐn

With layers of scented gossamers embroidered with phoenix tails,
I stitched a round bed canopy with light-green patterns deep into the night.
In dim moonlight, the round silk fan failed to hide my coyness for sure,
While amidst the rumblings of your cart, there was no way to talk to you.
Once I felt bereft in the growing gloom of a candle light
Without hearing from you, as the pomegranates were in blossom again.
Your dappled horse was tethered to weeping willows by the shore
And from where the southwest wind would come by, carrying me to see you?

# 無題（二）　　李商隱

昨夜星辰昨夜風，畫樓西畔桂堂東。
身無彩鳳雙飛翼，心有靈犀一點通。
隔座送鉤春酒暖，分曹射覆蠟燈紅。
嗟余聽鼓應官去，走馬蘭台類轉蓬。

# 無題（三）　　李商隱

來是空言去絕蹤，月斜樓上五更鐘。
夢為遠別啼難喚，書被催成墨未濃。
蠟照半籠金翡翠，麝熏微度繡芙蓉。
劉郎已恨蓬山遠，更隔蓬山一萬重！

# Untitled (No. 2)　Lǐ Shāng-yǐn

Last night, the sky was starlit with a fit of breeze
Along west of the painted tower and east of the cassia hall.
Even though we couldn't fly together like colorful phoenixes,
My heart still beats in consort with yours.
Sitting beside me, you passed on a hook and the spring wine was warm.
To guess the hidden object in red candle lights we teamed.
Alas! I heard the drum beating, reminding me the time to office,
And I rode my horse to the Secretariat, as rushing as tumbling weeds.

# Untitled (No. 3)　Lǐ Shāng-yǐn

The promise of your return was
As unsure as the knowing of where
You were. When the moon slanting o'er upstairs
And the bell ringing at the fifth watch,
The clarion of cocks failed to recall you back
In my dream. I hastened a letter
To you with its ink still wet. Embedded
With golden finches, a bed curtain was half
Draped in candle lights. Over the comforter
Broidered with lotus, the incense of musk lingered.
Once, Fellow Liu was embittered about the far
Distance of a fairy mountain, and we were even further
Apart beyond its infinite layers.

# 無題（四） 李商隱

颯颯東風細雨來，芙蓉塘外有輕雷。
金蟾齧鎖燒香入，玉虎牽絲汲井回。
賈氏窺簾韓掾少，宓妃留枕魏王才。
春心莫共花爭發，一寸相思一寸灰。

# 無題（五） 李商隱

重幃深下莫愁堂，臥後清宵細細長。
神女生涯原是夢，小姑居處本無郎。
風波不信菱枝弱，月露誰教桂葉香。
直道相思了無益，未妨惆悵是清狂。

# Untitled (No. 4)　Lǐ Shāng-yǐn

The rustling wind blows in drizzling rain from the east.

Rumbling beyond a lotus pond are imperceptibly wheels.

Burning incense is wafting through a door lock with a golden-toad.

Through a jade-tiger jigger, well-water is pulled up by hoisting ropes.

Peeking the young Hán thro a blind, Lady Jiǎ married him to her wishes.

Princess Fú left a bequest of cushion to Prince of Wèi for his talent.

Longing for you should never vie with dazzling blossom,

Lest longing for love is consumed inch by inch into ashes.


# Untitled (No.5)　Lǐ Shāng-yǐn

Awake from a sleep in a worry-free hall,

Where layers of curtains hang low, she finds

This sleepless night, quiet and endless like Fairy Queen's life,

Would make her a maiden without a mate.

Frail as cresses nodding in the wind and shivered by waves,

And, as bitter as cinnamon leaves with no moonlight and dews,

This lovesick, if it were of no reward,

Would turn a crazy heart into a glum mood.

# 瑤池　李商隱

瑤池阿母綺窗開，黃竹歌聲動地哀。
八駿日行三萬裡，穆王何事不重來？

# 賈生　李商隱

宣室求賢訪逐臣，賈生才調更無倫。
可憐夜半虛前席，不問蒼生問鬼神。

# The Jasper Lake Fairyland
## Lǐ Shāng-yǐn

By the Lake of Immortals, the Queen of Heaven opened carved windows,
Hearing all over the places the pathetic Song of Yellow-Bamboo.
Emperor Mu's eight steeds could travel ten thousand lis a day
And for what reason he won't return to visit her again?


# The Scholar Jiǎ    Lǐ Shāng-yǐn

Seeking advice from the virtuous, the Emperor
visited once-exiled courtier, Scholar Jiǎ,
whose talent and brilliance was unsurpassed.
Sat listening to him, the poor Emperor
leaned forward in thrill until midnight,
soliciting his views about ghosts
and spirits, but not about the populace.

# 蟬　李商隱

本以高難飽，徒勞恨費聲。
五更疏欲斷，一樹碧無情。
薄宦梗猶泛，故園蕪已平。
煩君最相警，我亦舉家清。

# 籌筆驛　李商隱

猿鳥猶疑畏簡書，風雲常為護儲胥。
徒令上將揮神筆，終見降王走傳車。
管樂有才原不忝，關張無命欲何如？
他年錦裡經祠廟，梁父吟成恨有餘。

# Cicada　Lǐ Shāng-yǐn

Unable to be well-fed from high trees,
Where regrettable is your neglected chirping
Now soft and lingering as dawn has approached,
You are even ignored in the shade of green trees.
As a petty official, my life is vagrant and unrooted
And weeds have already laid wild-waste to my ancestral home.
I am obliged to you for your most kind warning
And, like you, all my family live a frugal life too.


# A Marshal's Posthouse　Lǐ Shāng-yǐn

Apes and birds still have qualms about his army decrees
And fences of his fortress are often blessed by winds and clouds,
But even the Marshal, employing his divine forethought,
Couldn't save the doomed Lord driven away by a stagecoach.
What his talent, as excellent as Guǎn Zhòng and Lè Yì,
Could do after the sudden loss of Guān Yǔ and Zhāng Fēi?
Once, when walking past his temple at Brook of Brocade
I deplored his regrets for his lofty goal fallen through.

蟬
李商隱／籌筆驛　李商隱／133

# 錦瑟　李商隱

錦瑟無端五十弦，一弦一柱思華年。
莊生曉夢迷蝴蝶，望帝春心托杜鵑。
滄海月明珠有淚，藍田日暖玉生煙。
此情可待成追憶，只是當時已惘然。

# 為有　李商隱

為有雲屏無限嬌，鳳城寒盡怕春宵。
無端嫁得金龜婿，辜負香衾事早朝。

# A Luxurious Zither　Lǐ Shāng-yǐn

A luxurious zither, for no reason, has fifty strings,
And plucking each of them conjures up my spent prime.
In a morning dream, Zhuāng Zhōu was entranced to be a butterfly.
Emperor Wàng's nostalgia was echoed by a cuckoo's cry.
Merman's tears become pearls in blue oceans when the moon lights.
The veins of Blue Field jades are aired when the sun shines.
I am now able to recollect all such feelings,
Though I was truly at a loss in the old time.

# Lest He Misses Her　Lǐ Shāng-yǐn

There, behind a screen painted with clouds
An indescribable bonny lies,
Who is oft weary of the short-lived
Spring morning, as in the Capital
The winter has already gone.
Pointless, a high-ranking official
She has married, for he is obliged|
So much to attend the Court in dawn
As her flagrant bosom to belie.

# 春雨　李商隱

悵臥新春白袷衣，白門寥落意多違。
紅樓隔雨相望冷，珠箔飄燈獨自歸。
遠路應悲春晼晚，殘霄猶得夢依稀。
玉璫緘箚何由達，萬裡雲羅一雁飛。

# 涼思　李商隱

客去波平檻，蟬休露滿枝。
永懷當此節，倚立自移時。
北斗兼春遠，南陵寓使遲。
天涯占夢數，疑誤有新知。

# Rain in Spring    Lǐ Shāng-yǐn

In early spring, I once lay saddened in a white gown,
The tryst bleak and things often gone against my wish.
Your red chamber draped in rain appeared dreary.
In curtain-like drizzle, I returned alone as streetlight flickering.
Afar off, you would moan the passing of spring
And before the dawn had broken I would dream of you.
Hardly could jade earrings and love letters be sent to you,
Except by a wild goose flying o'er the thick, endless clouds.


# A Woeful Thought    Lǐ Shāng-yǐn

You have already departed, as waves souring to railings.
Branches are covered with dews and cicadas stop keening –
This is the moment I shall forever remember,
As I lean on the railing with time passed undetected.
I've been away from Cháng Ān for more than two springs,
And the messenger sent to Nán Líng has yet to return!
In a dream, I divine my future in a remote corner of the earth
And suspect you might have with a new friend acquainted.

# 風雨　李商隱

淒涼寶劍篇，羈泊欲窮年。
黃葉仍風雨，青樓自管弦。
新知遭薄俗，舊好隔良緣。
心斷新豐酒，消愁鬥幾千？

# Rain in the Wind    Lĭ Shāng-yĭn

Unlike the "Poem of a Rare Blade,"

I end up in pensive vein,

Trying to live out a life in vagrancy.

Leaves are withered and ruined by the rain

And the wind, while people in rich estates

Are indulging in entertainment music.

Slurs are cast upon new friends

And old acquaintances estranged

From each other. I fret out my days

Over Xīn Fēng liquor. Who cares how much I'd pay

For drinks to banish my anguish?

# 隋宮（一） 李商隱

乘興南遊不戒嚴，九重誰省諫書函。
春風舉國裁宮錦，半作障泥半作帆。

# 隋宮（二） 李商隱

紫泉宮殿鎖煙霞，欲取蕪城作帝家。
玉璽不緣歸日角，錦帆應是到天涯。
於今腐草無螢火，終古垂楊有暮鴉。
地下若逢陳後主，豈宜重問後庭花！

# The Suí's Palace (No. 1)　Lǐ Shāng-yǐn

Against remonstrance by his courtiers in the Court,
The King was on his feet to the South despite in harm's way,
So posh that half of the silks made in spring across
the land were cut into numnahs and half into sails.


# The Suí's Palace (No. 2)　Lǐ Shāng-yǐn

The Purple-Spring Palace is abandoned deep in misty haze,
And Emperor Yáng would rather select Yángzhōu to remain.
Were not his jade-like seal fallen to rebel's hand in dismay,
To the remote corner of the world would his dragon boat sail.
Amid rotten weeds hardly any firefly winks nowadays;
Over bending willows ravens are back in dusk as always.
Were the Emperor to meet Lord Zhāng in Sheol again,
It'd be ironic to seek erotic music be replayed!

# 北青蘿　李商隱

殘陽西入崦，茅屋訪孤僧。
落葉人何在，寒雲路幾層。
獨敲初夜磬，閒倚一枝藤。
世界微塵里，吾寧愛與憎。

# 登樂遊原　李商隱

向晚意不適，驅車登古原。
夕陽無限好，只是近黃昏．

# To a Green-vine Hut in North
## Lǐ Shāng-yǐn

As the sun declining behind the horizon
And leaves falling, I stroll through those winding paths
Surrounded by chilly clouds to visit a monk
Living alone in a hut, and try to spot him.
He percusses a chime stone alone in early night,
Leaning in relaxation against a vine branch.
Nothing in mundane world is as trivial as I,
Caring not a jot about loving and hatred.


# A Ride to an Ancient Tomb
## Lǐ Shāng-yǐn

My mood was troubled at dusk, but soothed
by a joy-ride to an ancient Tomb,
Where the sunset was in great wonder,
Though evening was getting closer.

# 宮詞　薛逢

十二樓中盡曉妝，望仙樓上望君王。
鎖銜金獸連環冷，水滴銅龍晝漏長。
雲髻罷梳還對鏡，羅衣欲換更添香。
遙窺正殿簾開處，袍褲宮人掃御床。

# 灞上秋居　馬戴

灞原風雨定，晚見雁行頻。
落葉他鄉樹，寒燈獨夜人。
空園白露滴，孤壁野僧鄰。
寄臥郊扉久，何年致此身？

# A Palace Poem    Xuē Féng

Those in Look-for-god Tower are all dressed up in early dawn
And those in Look-for-fairy Tower, eager for the king's favor to beg –
Favor, cold like chained door-locks embedded with golden animals
And long-delayed like endless drippings at night of a dragon clepsydra.
Bouncy and coiled hair combed again and again in the mirror
And silk wear dressed and changed again with added balm,
They peek at the imperial hall behind wide-opened curtains afar
And envy those well-dressed court maids making the king's bed.


# Autumn Life at Bà Plain    Mǎ Dài

The rain and the wind have lulled over Bà Plain,
Geese busy dashing in the sky as the sun starts to decline.
Amidst fallen leaves of trees in a strange land
And with lamps in the cold, I'm alone at night.
White dews drip in a deserted courtyard,
And a wild monk lives here next to a quiet wall.
I have lodged in this remote shack for a while
And when could I devote myself to my lord?

# 馬嵬坡　鄭畋

玄宗回馬楊妃死，雲雨難忘日月新。
終是聖明天子事，景陽宮井又何人？

# Mǎ Wēi Pō　Zhèng Tián

Returning from his flight and still in shock
By the tragedy of Lady Yáng's death,
Emperor Xuánzōng won't forget his past
Lewd life, while living a new life ahead.
His order to hang her, after all, was
Swift and clever that dwarfed Emperor Chén,
Who hid in a well to lament his fall.

# 菩薩蠻（詞組五首）　韋莊

## 首一

紅樓別夜堪惆悵，香燈半卷流蘇帳。殘月出門時，美人和淚辭。
琵琶金翠羽，絃上黃鶯語。勸我早歸家，綠窗人似花。

## 首二

人人盡說江南好，遊人只合江南老。春水碧於天，畫船聽雨眠。
壚邊人似月，皓腕凝霜雪。未老莫還鄉，還鄉須斷腸。

# Pú-sà mán (No.1-No.5)　Wéi Zhuāng

## No. 1

On that night of parting I felt rueful in a red chamber;

By a fragrant lamp, curtains with tassels were half-drawn.

When I departed,  waning was the moon

And a belle said goodbye to me in tears.

The strings of a lute with golden kingfisher feathers

Stroked a captivating note like an oriole,

Reminding me an early return,

And the dame by the green window was like a flower.

## No. 2

The South of Yangtze, they say, is a nice place,

Where wayfarers live a good life until old age.

The spring river is more blue-clear than the sky;

In a painted boat I could sleep, while rain drops.

The girl serving wine is as fair as the moon;

Her arms are as white as frost or frozen snow.

I won't repair to home while I am still young,

As returning home rives my heart with a deep sigh.

## 首三

如今卻憶江南樂，當時年少春衫薄。騎馬依斜橋，滿樓紅袖招。
翠屏金屈曲，醉入花叢宿。此度見花枝，白頭誓不歸。

## 首四

勸君今夜須沉醉，尊前莫話明朝事。珍重主人心，酒深情亦深。
須愁春漏短，莫訴金盃滿。遇酒且呵呵，人生能幾何。

## No. 3

The good times in the South I still ponder nowadays,
When I was a young lad wearing a spring silk-shirt.
By an arched bridge, while I was on a horseback,
Girls with red sleeves wooed me from a tower.
Amidst the glimmers of jade screens folded, I spent
My night drinking wine in a brothel while getting dazed.
This time when I meet my lady again, I'll never
Leave her, even if I become a grizzled man.

## No. 4

That you will get rotten tonight I pray
And forget about tomorrow with wine.
Try to treasure the host's intent, goodhearted
Like the wine in glass as deep as friendship.
In spring, I care about the fleeting night
And I'm lured to wine filled in a golden glass.
I have lived a shiftless life. Hooray! Hooray!
How long could my life be expected to last?

## 首五

洛陽城裡春光好，洛陽才子他鄉老。柳暗魏王堤，此時心轉迷。

桃花春水淥，水上鴛鴦浴。凝恨對殘暉，憶君君不知。

# 女冠子　韋莊

四月十七，正是去年今日。別君時，忍淚佯低面，含羞半斂眉。

不知魂已斷，空有夢相隨。除卻天邊月，沒人知。

## No. 5

In Luòyáng, where days are lovely in spring,
Great talents grow old in a strange land.
Hung low were willow twigs, shrouding
Over Prince Wèi's embankment;
And my mood turns dreary at this moment.
As peach flowers spread their blooms,
A pair of mandarin ducks is bathing
In a pool, its spring water in clear blue.
I gaze in great anxiety at the sunset,
Lest you don't know I'm still thinking of you.

# Nǔ-guàn zì　Wéi Zhuāng

On April the seventeenth,
Exactly a year ago to this day,
When I bade farewell to you,
I bent my head my choked tears to hide,
Half-frowned brows suffused
with coyness. No one cares about my
long-broken heart and the vain
merit of being with you in dreams,
except the moon beyond the sky.

# 章台夜思　韋莊

清瑟怨遙夜，繞弦風雨哀。
孤燈聞楚角，殘月下章台。
芳草已雲暮，故人殊未來。
鄉書不可寄，秋雁又南回。

# 金陵圖　韋莊

江雨霏霏江草齊，六朝如夢鳥空啼。
無情最自臺城柳，依舊煙籠十里堤。

# Brooding at Night in Terrace Tower
## Wéi Zhuāng

The faint notes of a lute were repining throughout

The night, its wailing strings lingering in the rain and breeze.

A Chǔ bugle was blowing, audible nearby a lone lamplight,

As beyond the Terrace Tower the moon declined.

Fair ladies were pining away like scattered clouds

And old friends already stopped coming by.

Letters to home were undelivered, as wild geese

Once more departed in fall for the South.


# A Bird's-eye View of Jinling
## Wéi Zhuāng

Along the river, the rain is in soft

Drizzle and the grass in a neat shape. Of all

The dreams of Six Dynasties nothing remains

But the chirping of birds. Shrouding in smog

The endless riverbank as before, they are the most

Indifferent of all – willows of the town of Tái.

# 書邊事　張喬

調角斷清秋，征人倚戍樓。
春風對青塚，白日落梁州。
大漢無兵阻，窮邊有客遊。
蕃情似此水，長願向南流。

# 已涼　韓偓

碧闌杆外繡簾垂，猩色屏風畫摺枝。
八尺龍須方錦褥，已涼天氣未寒時。

# Recording Frontier Affairs
## Zhāng Qiáo

Across the frontiers, where stands a tomb in grassy green
Amidst the breeze in the east and the sun dips deep
Into the west far beyond Liáng Zhōu,
Bugles are blowing in clear fall and soldiers
Are leaning at ease against watch towers.
As in this Great Kingdom of Hàn where peace
With no war has allured travelers to
Its remote frontiers, the tribal matter,
I pray, would run like a river that flows
As smooth as water to the south forever.


# The Crept-in Cold    Hán Wò

Embroidered blinds are dangling
Over green balusters and screens
In blood-red are painted with flowers
and branches. A new quilt in silk
Has just laid over an eight-feet
Rattan mat and now the chilly
Season has crept into feelings,
While yet to come is the winter.

# 除夜有作　崔塗

迢遞三巴路，羈危萬里身。
亂山殘雪夜，孤燭異鄉人。
漸與骨肉遠，轉於僮僕親。
那堪正飄泊，明日歲華新。

# 貧女　秦韜玉

蓬門未識綺羅香，擬託良媒益自傷。
誰愛風流高格調，共憐時世儉梳妝。
敢將十指誇針巧，不把雙眉鬥畫長。
苦恨年年壓金線，為他人作嫁衣裳。

# A Note on New Year's Eve　　Cuī Tú

With roads in Sān Bā stretching far and long,
I live a harsh life far away from home.
Amidst tumbled mountains with remains of snow,
I'm a lone stranger by a candle-light.
The farther apart with my kinsmen I'm
The more intimate with my houseboy I'm.
What's more saddening is a vagrant life
Facing another new year tomorrow.

# A Destitute Girl　　Qín Tāo-yù

Not used to the scent of silk scarf, I'm a poor girl
And shy of seeking a match by a match-maker.
Who prefers my elegant bearing and manner
To the cheap attire nowadays so widespread?
I boast more of my fingers good at needle-work
Than of my eyebrows penciled to vie with others'
And loathe embroidery work for others
With golden threads year after year for bridal dress.

除夜有作　崔塗／貧女　秦韜玉／161

# 寄人　張泌

別夢依依到謝家，小廊回合曲闌斜。
多情只有春庭月，猶為離人照落花。

# 菩薩蠻　無名氏

牡丹含露真珠顆，美人折向庭前過。含笑問檀郎，花強妾貌強。
檀郎故相惱，須道花枝好。一面發嬌嗔，碎挼花打人。

# A Note to You    Zhāng Mì

After you had left, your house loomed in my dream,
Its railings zig-zagged along a small, winding porch.
Only the moonlight came coating the spring court,
Still caressing those fallen flowers for me.

# Pú-sà mán    Author Unknown

Laden with drops of pearly dews, phonies
Were plucked by a belle who walked
Past a front courtyard, asking her
Lover with a smile: "Compared
to beauty, who would be better, the flower
Or me?" "As a beauty," in reply,
"There shall be no rival to the flower" –
He risked her ire on purpose. While
Flirting in pretense of irritation, she hit
Him with a piece of nipped-off flower.

# 雜詩　無名氏

近寒食雨草萋萋，著麥苗風柳映堤，
等是有家歸未得，杜鵑休向耳邊啼。

# 鵲踏枝　馮延巳

誰道閒情拋擲久？每到春來，惆悵還依舊。舊日花前常病酒，敢辭
鏡裡朱顏瘦。
河畔青蕪堤上柳，為問新愁，何事年年有？獨立小橋風滿袖，平林
新月人歸後。

# An Ad-lib Poem   Author Unknown

By Cool Food Festival, incessant was the rain
And the grass a lush green covered.
In the wind waved the wheat shoots
And along the riverbank swung the willows.
I felt like I could hardly embrace
The idea of going home,
And my ears could no longer
Bear the go-home coos of cuckoos.


# Què-tà zhī   Féng Yán-sì

Who says a wistful mind could be forsworn forever?
Every time when spring approaches,
The same remains my glum mood.
Drinking wine before flowers often makes me feel sick in days of yore,
And I couldn't care my red-cheeked face turned haggard in the mirror.
When tufted grass spreads along the river with willows on the riverbank,
What makes me fret about a renewed melancholy every year?
Full wind in my sleeves, I am standing alone on a small bridge,
And, after my return, the waxing moon lights over the woods.

# 相見歡　李煜

無言獨上西樓，月如鉤。寂寞梧桐深院，鎖清秋。剪不斷，理還亂，是離愁。別是一番滋味在心頭。

# 虞美人　李煜

春花秋月何時了，往事知多少。小樓昨夜又東風，故國不堪回首月明中。

雕欄玉砌應猶在，只是朱顏改。問君能有幾多愁，恰似一江春水向東流。

# Xiàng-jiàn huān　Lǐ Yù

I walk up to the West Pavilion alone,
While the crescent moon is fair.
The bleakness of autumn blankets a lonely parasol
In a quiet courtyard.
Unbroken while breaking,
Tangled while entangling
Is the wrench of my nostalgia –
It smacks of a different feeling in my heart.


# Yú-měi yén　Lǐ Yù

When will spring flowers and autumn moon be over?
How much could one still remember the past events?
Last night, the east wind again blew against the small tower;
In bright moonlight, I couldn't bear to sense my homeland.
Carved railings and marbled stairs should remain the same,
Though what has pinned away is the pride of my prime.
Tell me, how much stirred sorrows could I embrace
Like a river flowing to the east in springtime?

相見歡　李煜／虞美人　李煜／167

# 浪濤沙　李煜

往事只堪哀，對景難排。秋風庭院蘚侵階。一任珠簾閒不卷，終日誰來？

金鎖已沉埋，壯氣蒿萊。晚涼天淨月華開。想得玉樓瑤殿影，空照秦淮。

# 破陣子　李煜

四十年來家國，三千里地山河。鳳閣龍樓連雲霄，玉樹瓊枝作烟蘿，幾曾識干戈。

一旦歸為臣虜，沉腰潘鬢消磨。最是倉皇辭廟日，教坊猶奏別離歌，垂淚對宮娥。

# Làng-tāo shā　Lǐ Yù

The past is nothing but full of sorrow;

Facing the scene, I couldn't pull myself out of woe.

In autumn wind, moss ramps up the stairs of courtyard

And an array of beaded curtains remains unfurled.

All day long, no one would venture to come!

My golden sword is buried deep,

My aspired goals are perished like weeds.

In a chilly night, when in fair sky lights the moon,

I think of the façade of jade tower and its marbled hall

Reflecting idly in the water of Qin-huái River.

# Pò-zhèn zì　Lǐ Yù

A kingdom reigned by my family had lasted for two-score,

Its domain extended three thousand miles across mountains and rivers,

Up into the sky soared its phoenix-like pavilion and dragon-engraved tower.

Living among the precious trees of palace, as if in idyllic retreat,

I never had the chance to learn the cruelty of war.

Once being retained in confinement as a detainee,

With a thinner waistline and hoary hair I grew gaunt.

Most disconcerting was on the day of leaving my ancestral shrine in haste.

While the court musicians were still playing parting songs,

I succumbed to the onslaught of tears before palace maids.

# 渡中江望石城淚下　李煜

江南江北舊家鄉，三十年來夢一場。
吳苑宮闈今冷落，廣陵臺殿已荒涼。
雲籠遠岫愁千片，雨打歸舟淚萬行。
兄弟四人三百口，不堪閒坐細思量。

# 相見歡　李煜

林花謝了春紅，太匆匆。無奈朝來寒雨，晚來風。
胭脂淚，留人醉，幾時重。自是人生長恨水長東。

# Gazing in Tears at the Stone City,
# While Crossing the River    Lǐ Yù

In a native land stretched to the north and south

Of Yàng-zì River, for thirty years I have been

Living here like a dream. The inner chamber

Of palace in Wú Garden is deserted now,

And the stairs of palace hall in Quăng-líng

Must become desolate. As clouds shrouding

The distant mountains as endless as griefs,

And rains lashing against a homebound boat

As tearful as torrents, four brothers

And other three-hundred heads together

Couldn't bear sitting idly in deep thoughts.


# Xiàng-jiàn huān    Lǐ Yù

In spring blossom, a thicket of flowers seared

In frantic haste,

While unwillingly seized

by night wind and cold morning rain.

Rouge with tears

Ravished me,

And when could I expect you again?

Bitterness in life is as often as rivers bound to east.

渡中江望石城淚下　李煜／相見歡　李煜／171

# 浣溪沙　李煜

紅日已高三丈透，金爐次第添香獸。紅錦地衣隨步縐。
佳人舞點金釵溜，酒惡時拈花蕊嗅。別殿遙聞簫鼓奏。

# 一斛珠　李煜

曉粧初過，沈檀輕注些兒箇。向人微露丁香顆，一曲清歌，暫引櫻
桃破。
羅袖裛殘殷色可，杯深旋被香醪涴。繡床斜凭嬌無那，爛嚼紅茸，
向檀郎唾。

# Huàn-xī shà    Lǐ Yù

With the sun rising in the sky already
In a commanding height and incense added
To a golden censer in animal shape
Again and again, while red brocade
Carpets turned dimpled after dancing steps
And golden hairpins of dancers dropped,
Their toes twinkling, the Emperor, half-tipsy,
Sniffed plucked buds to come to his sense,
As flutes and drums playing in the court of a distant place.


# Yī-hú zhū    Lǐ Yù

She has just finished morning make-up
With lips rouged a bit,
Revealing her lilac-scented teeth.
Letting loose with a faint-toned melody,
She leisurely parts her ruby lips.
Her silk sleeves stained with a tiny bit of red wine,
Lips tinged with fragrant wine from a deep cup,
In carefree pretensions, she leans against an embroidered bed,
And chews a few red-fuzzy threads,
Spitting them on her flashy blade with a smile.

浣溪沙　李煜／一斛珠　李煜／1
7
3

# 菩薩蠻（一）　李煜

花明月暗籠輕霧，今宵好向郎邊去。剗襪步香階，手提金縷鞋。
畫堂南畔見，一向偎人顫。奴為出來難，教君恣意憐。

# 菩薩蠻（二）　李煜

蓬萊院閉天台女，畫堂晝寢人無語。拋枕翠雲光，繡衣聞異香。
潛來珠鎖動，驚覺銀屏夢。慢臉笑盈盈，相看無限情。

# Pú-sà mán (No.1)　Lǐ Yù

The mist light, the moon dim and flowers visible,
It's the night to go and see my lover.
Across fragrant steps I walked in stocking feet,
Carrying a pair of gilded shoes in my arm.
When I met you south of a painted hall,
Snuggling up against you, I was all of a dither.
It was rather difficult to be here for me,
Causing you to take an orgy of pity on me.

# Pú-sà mán (No.2)　Lǐ Yù

In a fairyland immured herself an angel,
Who quietly took a nap in a painted chamber,
Her hair, luxuriant and lucent, her pillows kept aside,
And a smell of rare scent from her embroidered gown.
He cat-walked there and turned a pearl-beaded door lock,
Waking her up behind a silver screen with a surprise,
And her graceful face was brimmed with smiles.
With immense affection they stared at each other.

# 菩薩蠻（三）李煜

銅簧韻脆鏘寒竹，新聲慢奏移纖玉。眼色暗相鉤，秋波橫欲流。
雨雲深繡戶，未便諧衷素。讌罷又成空，魂迷春夢中。

# Pú-sà mán (No.3)　Lǐ Yù

With the brass reed of a flute

blowing its sound bright,

her nimble fingers

deftly arching

to a new song,

they exchanged a sly look

at each other,

her bewitching eyes

shooting a burning look.

They tangled like the rain and clouds

in a lush room

their elevated feelings

mingled together at once

and turned unreal

after the royal feast –

his rave on her

wandering in an erotic dream.

# 浣溪沙　李璟

菡萏香銷翠葉殘，西風愁起綠波間。還與韶光共憔悴，不堪看。
細雨夢回雞塞遠，小樓吹徹玉笙寒。多少淚珠何限恨，倚欄杆。

# Huàn-xī shà   Lǐ Jǐng

The scent of lotus flowers wafted away,
Their green leaves withered, and sorrow furnished
By zephyr amidst blue ripples along with languished
Sweet time – all are deplorable to see.
In a drizzle, I wake up from a dream
About the faraway Jī-sài, playing notes
In a small tower until the jade flute turned cold.
With tears dropped in cascade
Much to my immense dismay,
I lean on a balustrade.

# 定風波　柳永

自春來，慘綠愁紅，芳心是事可可。日上花梢，鶯穿柳帶，猶壓香衾臥。暖酥消，膩雲嚲，終日厭厭倦梳裏。無那！恨薄情一去，音書無箇。

早知恁麼，悔當初，不把雕鞍鎖。向雞窗，只與蠻牋象管，拘束教吟課。鎮相隨，莫拋躲，針線閒拈伴伊坐，和我。免使年少，光陰虛過。

# Dìng-fēng bō    Lìu Yǎng

Since spring, leaves and flowers have pulled a glum face,
While I weary out the gloomy days.
The sun has risen over the heads of flowers
And orioles are fluttering among hanging willow twigs,
As I lounge in bed and covered by a flagrant quilt.
With a face gaunt
And hair disheveled and fallen,
All day long I am in no mood to freshen up,
For the insensible
Has left me,
With no message from him whatsoever.
Should I know that before,
I would lock up his carved saddle,
Bring him paper and ivory brush to his study,
Confining him to chanting poetry and reading
All day long without deserting me,
While I could snug up to him and do knitting works at leisure,
Lest the two of us dawdle away our youth.

# 滿江紅　柳永

萬恨千愁，將年少，衷腸牽繫。殘夢斷，酒醒孤館，夜長無味。可惜許枕前多少意，到如今兩總無終始。獨自箇，贏得不成眠，成憔悴。

添傷感，將何計，空只恁。厭厭地。無人處思量，幾度垂淚。不會得都來些子事，甚恁底死難拚棄。待到頭，終久問伊看，如何是。

# Mân-jiān hóng   Lìǔ Yǎng

With remorse and sorrow, so unceasing

And immeasurable in youth, I was burdened

With anxieties and my dream was interrupted

When I woke up from a dead-drunk in a quiet

Hospice with a long and blah night.

To my regret, much of the feelings

Cooed in bed between us ceased to exist.

The loss of sleep in languishment alone

Was what I gained. Saddened day by day,

Hard put to sadness, except leaving it alone in pains,

I couldn't help thinking of you when nobody was around

And I cried often, asking why there were things

So hard to forget until death? Somehow

I will surely ask you why it is so.

# 雨霖鈴　柳永

寒蟬淒切，對長亭晚，驟雨初歇。都門帳飲無緒，方留戀處、蘭舟催發。執手相看淚眼，竟無語凝噎。念去去、千里煙波，暮靄沈沈楚天闊。

多情自古傷離別，更那堪、冷落清秋節。今宵酒醒何處？楊柳岸、曉風殘月。此去經年，應是良辰好景虛設。便縱有，千種風情，更與何人說？

# Yù-lín líng　Lìǔ Yǎng

Cicadas in fall, their shrilling is doleful and short.

Across the ferry-house in the night

The shower has stopped at last.

In hum-drum, drinking in a tent by the city gate,

I hesitate to leave, as the ferryman reminds me to depart.

Hand in hand, when our spongy eyes gaze at each other,

We turn speechless with a choked throat, alas!

This trip across an endless misty waves

With evening smog hanging under the boundless Southern sky

Would make departure belie a tender love as always,

Let alone I dread an autumn season, bleak and unbearable.

Where shall I awake after a dead drunk tonight?

Along a riverbank, willows hang low,

As the moon is waning in twilight wind.

Those years after my departure would, if they were

Of a good time and a beautiful scenery, be in vain so

That even if so much more tender love now I embrace,

To whom should I pour out such a feeling?

雨霖鈴　柳永／185

# 八聲甘州　柳永

對蕭蕭暮雨灑江天，一番洗清秋。漸霜風淒緊，關河冷落，殘照當樓。是處紅衰翠減，苒苒物華休。唯有長江水，無語東流。
不忍登高臨遠，望故鄉渺邈，歸思難收。嘆年來蹤迹，何事苦淹留！想佳人、妝樓顒望，誤幾回、天際識歸舟。爭知我、依欄干處，正恁凝愁。

# Bā-shēn gān-zhōu　　Lìǔ Yǎng

In the sky the evening rain drops in sheet over the river,

Splashing the autumn into a fresh and chilly season.

The approaching wind is gusty and cold;

The mountain pass and the river are desolate,

As the sun, against the tower, is setting.

Everywhere flowers are wilting, leaves withering,

And wonderful scenes degenerate along with the time fleeting,

Except the water of the Yangtse River

That flows eastbound undisturbed.

I can't bear to climb and gaze far beyond the horizon,

Searching for my homeland, remote and blurred,

While a sense of nostalgia overtakes me.

I regret the wandering years I had of late,

Not knowing what makes me prolong my stay.

My fair lady looking out for me from her chamber

Has mistaken several times for my home-bound boat,

Unaware that while leaning against a balustrade,

I am so much beleaguered with grief.

# 夜半樂　柳永

凍雲黯淡天氣，扁舟一葉，乘興離江渚。渡萬壑千巖，越溪深處。怒濤漸息，樵風乍起，更聞商旅相呼。片帆高舉。泛畫鷁、翩翩過南浦。

望中酒旆閃閃，一簇煙村，數行霜樹。殘日下，漁人鳴榔歸去。敗荷零落，衰楊掩映，岸邊兩兩三三，浣沙遊女，避行客。含羞笑相

# Yè-bàn lè　Lìǔ Yǎng

A bleak sky with freezing clouds overhead,

I departed the riverbank in good spirit

On a lonely leaf-like boat,

Sailing past a myriad of valleys and cliffs

Across the deep waters of the Yuè River,

Where the surging waves gradually receded.

When suddenly flared up the tailwind,

I heard merchants and travelers cheering.

Its sail hauled up high to the wind,

And its prow painted with a fish-hawk,

The boat slid past the Southern Shore leisurely.

Well in sight were a wine shop's glimmering banner,

A tendril of smoke from a cluster of hamlets,

And a few rows of white trees.

When the sun was fading in the west,

Fishermen knocked their boats and returned.

While withered lotuses were scattered all around

And half-seen and half-hidden were waning willows,

Walking along the shore in twos or threes,

The silk-washing girls chuckled to each other,

Trying to shy away from travelers.

# 夜半樂（續）

到此因念，繡閣輕拋，浪萍難駐。嘆後約叮嚀竟何據？慘離懷、空恨歲晚歸期阻。凝淚眼、杳杳神京路。斷鴻聲遠長天暮。

# Yè-bàn lè (Cont'd.)

Once reached here, I remembered

Your decorated chamber being deserted unwittingly

And a vagrant life without roots.

Alas! The much-reminded reunion was ruined.

In a woeful nostalgia, I deplored the delay of return by year end.

My tears choked and in a remote distance the road to the capital loomed.

Beyond the sky in dusk the whining of a lonely goose echoed.

# 戚氏　柳永

晚秋天，一霎微雨灑庭軒。檻菊蕭疏，井梧凌亂，惹殘煙。淒然，望江關，飛雲黯淡夕陽間。當時宋玉悲感，向此臨水與登山。遠道迢遞，行人淒楚，倦聽隴水潺湲。正蟬吟敗葉，蛩响衰草，相應喧喧。

# Qī-shì　Liǔ Yǎng

On a late autumn day,

Drizzle sprinkled the courtyard in a trice

And fenced chrysanthemums were faded.

Nearby a well, the rambling leaves of parasols

Were scattered in a wisp of smoke.

In sorrow and grief,

I gazed at the River Pass afar;

The louring clouds scudding in the setting sun

Once made Sòng Yù feel doleful here.

This river-paddling and mountain-climbing

Along with a journey, remote and far away,

Made me, like travelers in dismal conditions,

Tired of listening to the rippling of Lǒng River.

Cicadas chirped among dying leaves

And crickets creaked in withered grasses,

As if both echoing raucously against one another.

# 戚氏（續）

孤館度日如年。風露漸變，悄悄至更闌。長天淨，絳河清淺，皓月蟬娟。思綿綿。夜永對景，那堪屈指，暗想從前。未名未祿，綺陌紅樓，往往經歲遷延。

# Qī-shì (Cont'd.)

A day dallied away in a quiet hospice was like a year.

The wind and dews were changing,

As the time crept past the midnight,

The deep empyrean, crystal-like,

The milky way, in pellucid clarity,

And the fair moon, gracious and lucent.

In endless thinking,

With such a scene all night in front of me,

I couldn't stand reckoning up what I did,

Reminiscing the past

When I was obscure with no high position attained,

Frequently roving on red towers

Across the crossroads for years.

# 戚氏（續）

帝里風光好，當年少日，暮宴朝歡。況有狂朋怪侶，遇當歌、對酒
競留連。別來迅景如梭，舊游似夢，煙水程何限！念利名憔悴長縈
絆，追往事、空慘愁顏。漏箭移、稍覺輕寒。漸嗚咽、畫角數聲
殘。對閒窗畔，停燈向曉，抱影無眠。

# Qī-shì (Cont'd.)

The capital, its scenery was charming,

When I was young,

Feasting away day and night in conviviality,

More so with crazy friends and weird fellows,

All singing and drinking together, reluctant to leave.

Since I had left, time fled as fast as a weaver's shuttle.

The trip I made before was like a dream,

Its river tours misty and never-ending.

Contemplating fortune and fame often haunted me in languishment.

Thinking of the past left me in a hopeless despair with a gloomy face.

The indicator-rod of a hourglass was changing as the weather turned chilly,

And the blare of a painted bugle was moaning as it tapered off to a close.

Nearby the window pane nothing stirred,

And a burnt light cracked the first shade at dawn,

While I huddled my shadow without a sleep.

# 歸朝歡　柳永

別岸扁舟三兩隻。葭葦簫簫風淅淅。沙汀宿雁破烟飛、溪橋殘月和霜白。漸漸分曙色。路遙山遠多行役。往來入、隻輪雙槳、盡是利名客。

一望鄉關烟水隔。轉覺歸心生羽翼。愁雲恨雨兩牽縈、新春殘臘相催逼。歲華都瞬息。浪萍風梗誠何益。歸去來、玉樓深處、有個人相憶。

# Guī-cháo huān  Lìŭ Yăng

A few lonely boats were over the shore

With reeds rustling and wind whistling,

As geese marooning on sand islets burst out through the mists;

The bridge of brook was covered with snow-white frost,

While dawn was peeping through the waning moon.

From the distant mountains across the roads afar,

Travelers shuttled to and fro

In two-wheel carts and two-paddle boats,

All pursuing fame and wealth alike.

Gazing at my home town across the misty river,

I felt like on the wing upon the thought of going home.

About us prowled the worrisome clouds and the incessant rain.

Early spring hustled the year-end to pass in haste,

And the fleeting time pressed hard.

What's the use to be a vagrant drifting like duckweeds and swinging stems?

I ought to leave for my home town

And see the one secluded oneself in a jade tower,

Longing for me.

# 鬻鹽歌　柳永

煮海之民何所營，婦無蠶織夫無耕。
衣食之源太寥落，牢盆煮就汝輪征。
年年春夏潮盈浦，潮退刮泥成島嶼。
風乾日曝鹹味加，始灌潮波熘成鹵。
鹵濃城淡未得閒，采樵深入無窮山。
豹蹤虎跡不敢避，朝陽山去夕陽還。
船載肩擎未遑歇，投入巨灶炎炎熱。
晨燒暮爍堆積高，才得波濤變成雪。

# A Song of Sea-water Brewers
# Lìǔ Yǎng

Unable were sea-water brewers to toil their hands for a living,

Their wives no silks to weave and husbands no crops to reap,

Their resources of livelihood too meagre to pay tax

But brewing sea-water with a pan.

In each spring and summer, when along the shore the tide was high,

Mud slurry of the receding tide was scraped up into sand dunes –

Their salting increased when dried by the wind and baked by the sun –

Rinsed before long by sea water and cleansed into sea brine.

No sooner they were busy sampling the consistency of salt content

Than they would go deep into mountains to gather timers,

Ignoring the tracks left behind by leopards and tigers,

As they went to the mountains in the morning and returned after sunset,

Hurried with logs on their shoulders that were carried back by boats

And were thrown into a huge stove burning in blazing

Hot from dawn till evening, turning tossing waves

Finally into white salt piled in decked heaps.

# 鬻鹽歌（續）

自從瀦鹵至飛霜，無非假貸充餱糧。
秤入官中得微直，一緡往往十緡償。
周而復始無休息，官租未了私租逼。
驅妻逐子課工程，雖作人形俱菜色。

# A Song of Sea-water Brewers (Cont'd.)

They produced fine salt from sea brine,

Trying to make both ends meet through a loan.

The paltry earnings from sale pegged to an official rate

Were hardly able to pay off their usury -

Ten times the total earnings received.

Year after year, they toiled round the clock without rest,

With payments of taxes outstanding and private loans unpaid.

Their wives and children were compelled to join the work

And their gaunt body all drawn with a wan complexion.

# 鬻鹽歌（續）

鬻海之民何苦門，安得母富子不貧。
本朝一物不失所，願廣皇仁到海濱。
甲兵淨洗征輪輟，君有餘財罷鹽鐵。
太平相業爾惟鹽，化作夏商周時節。

# A Song of Sea-water Brewers (Cont'd.)

They spent their harsh lives of toil and moil in salterns.

How could a rich state allow its citizens in poverty?

They should all be in their element under this dynasty.

May the Emperor's benevolence be extended to seashores.

When war is avoided and people are exempted from military tours,

The Emperor would have the surplus to avoid taxes on iron and salt.

A beatific peace sought by the premier rests with an exemption of salt tax

That would turn the dynasty into the full pride of Xià, Shāng and Zhōu.

# 蝶戀花　歐陽修

六曲欄杆偎碧樹。楊柳風輕，展盡黃金縷。誰把鈿箏移玉柱？穿簾燕子雙飛去。

滿眼游絲兼落絮。紅杏開時，一霎清明雨。濃睡覺來鶯亂語。驚殘好夢無尋處。

# 杏花　王安石

石梁度空曠，茅屋臨清炯。
俯窺嬌饒杏，未覺身勝影。
嫣如景陽妃，含笑墮宮井。
怊悵有微波，殘妝壞難整。

# Dié-liàn huā　Ōu-Yang Xiū

A winding balustrade clings to green trees;
Willows hanging in breeze
Show all their branches like golden threads.
Who is tuning a gilded zither with jade frets,
Making two swallows fly past curtains and scour away?
Dangling cobwebs and falling catkins to my eyes display.
As red apricots spreading their blooms,
And rain starts in Tome-Sweeping season.
Awaken out of a deep sleep to the twittering of warblers,
How could I recall a sweet dream awfully disturbed?

# An Apricot Flower　Wáng Ān-shí

A stone bridge arches over the broad expanse of water,
And a thatched hut nearby a clear and glittering river
Peeks down an apricot flower, charming and tender,
Unaware of its beauty outshining its image in the water.
Sweet as the Lady of Jǐng-yáng Palace,
Who, while smiling, hides herself in a well of the palace,
The apricot flower is saddened with the crisp waves
That spoils its make-up, which is hard to adjust again.

# 江城子　蘇軾

夢中了了醉中醒，只淵明，是前生。走偏人間，依舊卻躬耕。昨夜東坡春雨足，烏鵲喜，報新晴。

雪堂西畔暗泉鳴，北山傾，小溪橫。南望亭丘，孤秀聳曾城。都是斜川當日境，吾老矣，寄餘齡。

# Jiāng-chéng zì    Sū Shì

As clear in dreams and awake in drunk

As Yuān Míng,

Who, like an avatar, lived my pre-life,

I have gone through all the vicissitudes of life

And end up with a true farmer.

Last night at Eastern Slope where spring rain abundant,

Black magpies were cheerful,

Heralding a refreshed fine day.

By the west of Snow Hall,

hidden behind a murmuring rill,

An inverted North Mountain reflecting

In the stream flowing across the surface,

And to the south, a pavilion in Céng Chéng rising

High above the town of Xié Brook,

In solitude and elegance –

All are the scenes same as in ancient days.

My days are past the best. And I wish

To live out my declining years here.

# 送鄭戶曹　蘇軾

水遠彭祖樓，山圍西馬台。
古來豪傑地，千歲有餘哀。
隆準飛上天，重瞳亦成灰。
白門下呂布，大星隕臨淮。
尚想劉德輿，置酒此徘徊。
邇來苦寂寞，廢圃多蒼苔。
河從百步响，山到九里回。
山水自相激，夜聲轉風雷。
蕩蕩清河壖，黃樓我所開。
秋月墮城角，春風搖酒杯。
遲君為坐客，新詩出瓊瑰。

# Seeing off Financial Officer Zhèng
## Sū Shì

The Péng-zǔ Tower surrounded by rivers

And the Racing-horse Platform encircled by mountains

Were places for gallant warriors since ancient times,

Long remaining pathetic for thousand years.

Nose-arched Emperor Liú Bāng rose to heaven,

And Ziàng Yǔ, double-pupil in his eyes, turned into ashes too,

While Lǚ Bù was beheaded at the White Gate,

And the Lord of Lín-huái died when a big star fell.

In recollection, Emperor Liú-dē Yú

Once hung around here, throwing parties.

Lately, I am burdened by loneliness,

Letting garden unattended with deep green moss.

Waters from Bǎi-bù lashed rumbling

Against mountains and winding back

from Jiǔ-lǐ, while the sound of wind

And thunder went peeling through the night.

Qīng-hé rolled along the riparian land,

And the Yellow Tower was built under my supervision.

The autumn moon declined over the corner of city-wall.

Spring wind shook the wine glass,

While I was waiting for you to be my guest,

And a new verse was transformed from exquisite lines.

# 送鄭戶曹（續）

樓成君已去，人事固多乖。
他年君倦游，白首賦歸來。
登樓一長嘯，使君安在哉。

# Seeing off Financial Officer Zhèng (Cont'd.)

Just as the tower was built, you were long gone.

Life is full of events tangential to our desires.

When you are tired of being a vagrant

And sing "Home Again" with a hoary head,

 You would climb up the tower with a long howl,

Asking, "Sir, where can you be?"

# 寄子由（摘自中秋月寄子由三首）
# 蘇軾

悠哉四子心，共此千里明。
明月不解老，良辰難合并。
四顧坐上人，聚散如流萍。
嘗聞此宵月，萬里同陰晴。
天公自著意，此會那可輕。
明年各相望，俯仰今古情。

# To Zǐ Yó[1]   Sū Shì

The hearts of four of us are content and feel at ease,
Sharing together the moonlight thousands of miles afar.
The bright moon does not understand why we grow old
And good moment could hardly be enjoyed by us all.
When I recollect guests dinning together before,
Gatherings and separations appear like drifting duckweeds.
Once I heard that tonight's moon, dull or bright,
Is the same across thousands of miles apart.
Our Lord does bless us all
And we cannot take this gathering lightly.
Next year each of us shall look at the moon,
Mulling over events transpired now and before.

---

[1]   From a collection of three poems composed on Mid-autumn Day.

# 紅梅　蘇軾

怕愁貪睡獨開遲，自恐冰容不入時。
故作小紅挑杏色，尚餘孤瘦雪霜姿。
寒心未肯隨春態，酒暈無端上玉肌。
詩老不知梅格在，更看綠葉與青枝。

# 木蘭花令　蘇軾

梧桐葉上三更雨。驚破夢魂無覓處。
夜涼枕簟已知秋，更聽寒蛩促機杼。
夢中歷歷來時路。猶在江亭醉歌舞。
尊前必有問君人，為道別來心與緒。

# Red Plum    Sū Shì

Wearied by worries and somnolence, she bloomed alone late.
Concerned about her frosty face being out of fashion,
She turned it on purpose into a small peach-and-apricot-like color,
Her lanky stems remained in snow-white manner.
Her chilling heart declined her bearing in spring.
A blush willy-nilly vermillioned her lily-white skins.
The Master of poetry didn't know the true essence of plum,
Paying attention only to her green leaves and young branches.

# Mù-lán huā-lìng    Sū Shì

The rainy swill of parasol leaves ruins
By surprise a fine dream of mine
That nowhere else I could find.
Lying on a bamboo mat reveals
The arrival of autumn on a cold night, and I hear
Crickets keening, urging weavers to weave.
I kept in my dream a journey I took
Before with vivid details, singing and dancing
In a river-pavilion while dazed with drinks.
Before the wine jar, there must be someone
Who cares for you, asking your mood
And feeling since our parting.

# 念奴嬌　蘇軾

大江東去，浪淘盡，千古風流人物。故壘西邊，人道是，三國周
郎赤壁。亂石穿空，驚濤拍岸，捲起千堆雪。江山如畫，一時多
少豪傑！

遙想公瑾當年，小喬初嫁了，雄姿英發。羽扇綸巾，談笑間，強虜
灰飛煙滅。故國神遊，多情應笑我，早生華髮，人間如夢，一尊還
酹江月。

# Niàn-nú jiāo   Sū Shì

The great river running eastward, its waves
have swept away luminaries renowned for ages.
On the west of the old rampart, they said,
Is the Red Cliff ruled by General Zhōu of the Three Kingdoms,
Where a strewn mass of peaks soaring high up into the air
With bursting surges lashing the shores,
Like whirling up thousands of heaps of snow.
Here, as scenic as a painting,
Was the realm once full of splendid heroes!
I recollect when Zhōu Yú married the younger Qiáo,
He was in his prime and in a crust of gallantry.
With a feather fan and in a silk head-scarf,
He spoke in smiles, while making his mighty rivals
Burned into writhing ashes and vanished in smokes.
Mocked for being emotional, I glide into a deep thinking
of my home land, wearing hoary hair already,
and living like a dream in this world of mortals.
I pour out a libation to the bright moon in river.

# 水調歌頭　蘇軾

明月幾時有？把酒問青天。不知天上宮闕，今夕是何年。我欲乘風歸去，又恐瓊樓玉宇，高處不勝寒。起舞弄清影，何似在人間！轉朱閣，低綺戶，照無眠。不應有恨，何事長向別時圓？人有悲歡離合，月有陰晴圓缺，此事古難全。但願人長久，千里共嬋娟。

# Shuǐ-diào gē-tóu    Sū Shì

With a cup of wine, I ask the blue sky:
"When the moon will be bright again,
And in which year of the imperial palace
In heaven falls tonight?" I wish to go home
By the wind, though high in the splendid palace
Of the moon I won't stand its cold.
I start dancing amidst my visible shadows,
As if out of this world.
The moon, its light casts around a red tower, sifting
Past emblazoned windows, and makes me feel sleepless.
There shouldn't be any regret, but why
You wax only when we are parting?
Things like sorrow and joy, departure
And reunion to men, or shade and bright,
Wax and wane to the moon, could never be
Certain since time immemorial. I wish indeed
We could all live long enough to taste
The beauty of the moon together,
While being thousands of miles away.

# 水龍吟　蘇軾

似花還似非花，也無人惜從教墜。拋家傍路，思量卻是，無情有思。縈損柔腸，困酣嬌眼，欲開還閉。夢隨風萬里，尋郎去處，又還被，鶯呼起。
不恨此花飛盡，恨西園，落紅難綴。曉來雨過，遺踪何在？一池萍碎。春色三分，二分塵土，一分流水。細看來，不是楊花點點，是離人淚。

# Shuǐ-lóng yín    Sū Shì

Catkins seemed like as much of flowers as of non-flowers

Are wafting casually, to no one's taste,

Across the roadside, away from their roots,

And yet couldn't help pondering

In deep thoughts with no feelings.

Her sorrows beleaguered like weeping willows

And her sleepy, lovely eyes, like willow leaves,

Barely open before closed,

She follows the wind in a dream to reach

Her lover thousands of miles away,

Only to be awakened by oriels' twittering.

Nothing should be sorry for the blown-away flowers,

Except those fallen and scattered in the Western Garden.

When the dawn peeks and the rain has stopped,

How could one trace the tracks of their remains?

Upon a closer look, shrunk catkins in a pool of springtime

Filled mainly with dust and partly with flowing water,

Do not appear like specks, rather the tears of a parting partner.

# 八聲甘州　蘇軾

有情風萬里卷潮來，無情送潮歸。問錢塘江上，西興浦口，幾度斜暉？不用思量今古，俯仰昔人非。誰似東坡老，白首忘機。

記取西湖西畔，正春山好處，空翠烟霏。算詩人相得，如我與君稀。約他年，東還海道，願謝公雅志莫相違。西州路，不應回首，為我沾衣。

# Bā-shēn gān-zhōu    Sū Shì

There, at the Xī-xīng Bay
Of the Qián-táng River,
Where miles of miles of tidal waves
Were rolled over by a kind wind
And then subsided and held back
By a careless wind, frequented we
in the slant rays of a sinking-sun.
It's useless to wrestle with the present
And the past, mulling over the wrong-doings
Of our forefathers. Who will become a grizzled
Old man like Dōng-pō, shrugging
Off the pursuit of fame and wealth?
The scenery, west of the West Lake,
Unfolds the attractions of Spring Mountain
That lies shrouded in fog and far-folded mists.
Thinking of the suave acquaintance
Among poets, the profound friendship
Between you and me is rare. Let's
Hope someday we will return
From the east through a sea-way,
In keeping with Lord Xiè's refined spirit.
Along the road to the west county,
Don't look back and cry for me.

# 浣溪沙　周邦彥

樓上晴天碧四垂，樓前芳草接天涯。勸君莫上最高梯。
新筍已成堂下竹，落花都上燕巢泥。忍聽林表杜鵑啼。

# Huān-xī shā　Zhōu Bāng-yàng

Upstairs, a clear blue light sprinkled down from the sky
With green grass in front of the tower reaching the horizon afar,
I pray, up to the dazzling highest step, you won't climb.
With new shoots already grown into bamboos by the hall
And fallen flowers turned into the soils of swallow's nest,
How can I bear to listen to cuckoos' trills beyond the forest?

卷五 譯詩中文
（Poems Translated from English into Chinese）

# That Time of Year Thou May'st in Me Behold[1]
## —William Shakespeare (1564-1616)

That time of year thou may'st in me behold,

When yellow leaves, or none, or few, do hang

Upon those boughs which shake against the cold,

Bare ruin'd choirs where late the sweet birds sang.

In me thou see'st the twilight of such day

As after sunset fadeth in the west,

Which, by and by, black night doth take away,

Death's second self, that seals up all in rest.

In me thou see'st the glowing of such fire

That on the ashes of his youth doth lie,

As the death-bed whereon it must expire,

Consum'd with  that which it was nourish'd by.

This thou perceiv'st, which makes thy love more strong,

To love that well which thou must leave ere long.

---

[1] Shakespeare's Sonnet #73.

# 不久你將覺察我[1]
## ——威廉·莎士比亞（1564-1616）

不久你將覺察我，
零星枯葉掛枝上，
枝葉哆嗦向寒躲，
向晚群鳥嘰喳啼。
不久你將覺察我，
你覺我已臨黃昏，
恰似斜陽已西蝕，
旋即黑夜替而代，
死亡替身即圓寂。
你覺我情仍洋溢，
雖我青春今已喪，
此情因愛而憔悴，
奈何情斷臨終床！
你察此理情益深，
即將分手情應長。

---

[1] 莎士比亞十四行詩，第七十三首。

# The Expense of Spirit[1]
## —William Shakespeare (1564-1616)

The expense of spirit in a waste of shame

Is lust in action; and till action, lust

Is perjured,  murderous, bloody, full of blame,

Savage, extreme, rude, cruel, not to trust;

Enjoy'd no sooner but despised straight,

Past reason hunted, and no sooner had

Past reason hated, as a swallow'd bait

On purpose laid to make the taker mad;

Mad in pursuit and in possession so;

Had, having, and in quest to have, extreme;

A bliss in proof, and proved, a very woe;

Before, a joy proposed; behind, a dream.

All this the world well knows; yet none knows well

To shun the heaven that leads men to this hell.

---

[1]  Shakespeare's Sonnet #129.

# 精力之消耗[1]
## ——威廉·莎士比亞（1564-1616）

消耗精力而徒使慚愧
是屬一再追求情慾。
情慾是作假、謀害，血腥，充滿指斥，
野蠻，極端、粗魯、殘忍、互悖；
享受情慾一旦滿足，隨即逕自受到卑視，
求得以往的緣由，
旋即又憎恨以往的緣由，猶如故意
置餌於人口中，使食者發瘋、
狂於追求，狂於佔有；
情慾已達，正在追求及努力追求，三者皆屬縱慾；
正在求證至樂，且證明是至樂，其實是悲痛。
至樂之前是逗樂，至樂之後留下一夢。
這些世人皆知，但沒人洞悉
如何避免導致這種罪惡的極樂。

---

[1] 莎士比亞十四行詩，第一百廿九首。

# The Rape of the Lock[1]
## —Alexander Pope (1688-1744)

Not with more glories, in th' etherial plain,

The sun first rises o'er the purpled main,

Than, issuing forth, the rival of his beams

Launch'd on the bosom of the silver Thames.

Fair nymphs, and well-dress'd youths around her shone,

But ev'ry eye was fix'd on her alone.

On her white breast a sparkling cross she wore,

Which Jews might kiss, and infidels adore.

Her lively looks a sprightly mind disclose,

Quick as her eyes, and as unfix'd as those:

Favours to none, to all she smiles extends;

Oft she rejects, but never once offends.

Bright as the sun, her eyes the gazers strike,

And, like the sun, they shine on all alike.

Yet graceful ease, and sweetness void of pride,

Might hide her faults, if belles had faults to hide:

If to her share some female errors fall,

Look on her face, and you'll forget 'em all.

---

[1]　From Canto II, 1-18.

# 鬈髮遇劫記[1]
## ——亞歷山大·蒲柏（1688-1744）

從飄渺的空中，
先在紫色的海上升起的太陽，
與其落在粼粼的泰晤士河中
所射出的爭艷光芒，二者同樣燦爛。
漂亮的女孩及衣著考究的年輕人亮現在她身旁，
大家的眼光都被她所吸引著。
她乳白的胸前戴著一枚閃光的十字架，
猶太人或會吻它，異教徒或會讚美它。
她生動的外表露出活潑的心靈，
伶俐但不專注，猶如她的眼睛；
她不青睞任何人，但笑迎眾人；
她常推卻，但絕不冒犯。
眼睛像太陽般明亮，投向注視她的人，
而眼光像太陽一般照耀大家。
但優雅安逸、甜而不傲
許能掩飾她的缺點，假定美女有錯可藏：
設如僅女人有的錯誤怪在她份上的話，
那末注視她的臉，你會忘了她所有的過錯。

---

摘自第二章，前十八行。

# The Echoing Green
## —William Blake (1757-1827)

The Sun does arise

And make happy the skies.

The merry bells ring

To welcome the Spring.

The skylark and thrush,

The birds of the bush,

Sing louder around

To the bell's cheerful sound,

While our sport shall be seen

On the Echoing Green.

Old John with white hair

Does laugh away care,

Sitting under the oak,

Among the old folk.

They laugh at our play,

And soon they shall say:

"Such, such were the joys,

When we all, girls and boys,

In our youth time were seen

On the Echoing Green."

# 回響草地
## ——威廉・布萊克（1757-1827）

太陽已上升，
氣候宜人。
悅耳的鐘鳴聲
迎接著春天。
灌木林中
之雲雀及歌鶇，
和著悅耳的鐘聲，
在附近愈發的高聲啼唱；
那時在迴響的草地上，
將會看到我們遊戲。
白髮斑斑的老約翰
總是對煩惱一笑了之；
與其他老人，
一起坐在橡樹下。
不一會，他們譏笑我們玩樂
而說：「像這樣的歡樂，
在我們是年輕的男、
女孩子的時候，
同樣可在
迴響草地上看到。」

# The Echoing Green (Cont'd.)

Till the little ones, weary,

No more can be merry;

The sun does descend,

And our sports have an end.

Round the laps of their mothers

Many sisters and brothers,

Like birds in their nest,

Are ready for rest,

And sport no more seen

On the darkening Green.

# 回響草地（續）

直到小傢伙們疲倦
而不再歡樂；
太陽已下山，
遊戲已結束。
很多兄弟姐妹們，
圍繞在母親膝旁，
像巢中的鳥，
準備休息。
而在漸暗的草地上，
再也看不到嬉戲。

# "To See a World…"[1]
## —William Blake (1757-1827)

To see a World in a Grain of Sand
And a Heaven in a Wild Flower,
Hold Infinity in the palm of your hand
And Eternity in an hour.

# Ah, Sunflower
## —William Blake (1757-1827)

Ah, Sunflower, weary of time,
　　Who countest the steps of the Sun;
Seeking after that sweet golden clime
　　Where the traveler's journey is done;

Where the Youth pined away with desire,
　　And the pale Virgin shrouded in snow,
Arise from their graves, and aspire
　　Where my Sunflower wishes to go!

---

[1] From his "Auguries of Innocence."

# 〈瞻世界…〉<sup>1</sup>

— 威廉・布萊克（1757-1827）

瞻世界之於細沙，眇蒼穹若蓄野花。
持無窮置汝手掌，促萬古之於剎那。


# 啊，向日葵

— 威廉・布萊克（1757-1827）

啊，向日葵，對時間不耐煩，
　　算著時間的推移；
尋求討人喜愛的地方
　　那兒旅客行程已畢；

那兒因慾望而憔悴的年輕人，
　　及埋在雪中的蒼白處女，
皆從墓中而起，嚮往
　　向日葵欲往的去處！

_____

詩人《Auguries of Innocence》一詩。

# Composed upon Westminster Bridge[1]
## —William Wordsworth (1770-1850)

Earth has not anything to show more fair:

    Dull would he be of soul who could pass by

    A sight so touching in its majesty:

This City now doth like a garment wear

The beauty of the morning; silent, bare,

    Ships, towers, domes, theatres, and temples lie

    Open unto the fields, and to the sky;

All bright and glittering in the smokeless air.

Never did sun more beautifully steep

    In his first splendour valley, rock, or hill;

Ne'er saw I, never felt, a calm so deep!

    The river glideth at his own sweet will:

Dear God! the very houses seem asleep;

    And all that mighty heart is lying still!

---

[1] Composed on September 3, 1803.

# 威斯敏斯特橋上所作[1]
## ——威廉·華茲華斯（1770-1850）

世上沒有更悅目的景象：

  只有笨人才會過而不視

  這令人感動的盛景：

清晨之美覆蓋著

倫敦；寂靜，樸質，

  船，塔，圓頂建築，戲院及教堂

  皆躺在遠處，伸向天邊；

在晴朗的空中光亮閃爍。

初晨太陽的壯觀，從沒如此

  美麗的洋溢在山谷及丘岩上；

如此深深的寧靜，我從未曾見過及體會過！

  河水悠閒自流：

天啊！大家都仍在入睡；

  城市的偉大活力仍未甦醒！

---

[1] 作於1803年9月3日。

# I Wandered Lonely as a Cloud
## —William Wordsworth (1770-1850)

I wandered lonely as a cloud
That floats on high o'er vales, and hills,
When all at once I saw a crowd,
A host, of golden daffodils;
Beside the lake, beneath the trees,
Fluttering and dancing in the breeze.

Continuous as the stars that shine
And twinkle on the milky way,
They stretched in never-ending line
Along the margin of a bay:
Ten thousand saw I at a glance,
Tossing their heads in the sprightly dance.

The waves beside them danced; but they
Out-did the sparkling waves in glee: –
A poet could not but to gay,
In such a jocund company:
I gazed – and gazed – but little thought
What wealth the show to me had brought.

# 獨自徜徉雲間
## ——威廉・華茲華斯（1770-1850）

我隻身徘徊，像一朵浮雲，
高高的飄越山谷及丘陵；
倏然，看到一叢又一叢
帶金黃色的水仙花，
在湖邊及樹下，
飄動飛舞在微風中。

像光亮的星星
綿延在銀河裡閃閃發光，
水仙花沿著海灣邊，
一望無際的一線伸展，
一瞥眼，我看到成千萬花朵，
甩著頭、輕快的跳著舞。

花旁的浪花跳著舞；
但花比閃光的浪花愈發跳得興奮：—
詩人不禁感到喜悅
與這樣的歡樂為伍：
我注視又注視，但很少想到
這盛景已為我帶來的好處。

# I Wandered Lonely as a Cloud (Cont'd.)

For oft, when on my couch I lie

In vacant and in pensive mood,

They flesh upon that inward eye

Which is the bliss of solitude,

And then my heart with pleasure fills,

And dances with the daffodils.

# 獨自徜徉雲間（續）

因為，每每當我躺在沙發上，
在清閑及沈思的心情下，
水仙花滋養著我的心靈，
那是靜處的最高享樂，
然後我心中充滿著喜悅，
一起和水仙花共舞。

# In the Churchyard at Cambridge
## —Henry Wadsworth Longfellow (1807-1882)

In the village churchyard she lies,
Dust is in her beautiful eyes,
   No more she breathes, nor feels, nor stirs;
At her feet and at her head
Lies a slave to attend the dead,
   But their dust is white as hers.

Was she a lady of high degree,
So much in love with the vanity
   And foolish pomp of this world of ours?
Or was it Christian charity,
And lowliness and humility,
   The richest and rarest of all dowers?

Who shall tell us?  No one speaks;
No color shoots into those cheeks,
   Either of anger or of pride,
At the rude question we have asked;
Nor will the mystery be unmasked
   By those who are sleeping at her side.

# 劍橋的墓地裡
## ——亨利・沃茲沃思・朗費羅（1807-1882）

她躺在村中的墓地裡，
屍骨之美在於她的眼睛，
　她不再呼吸，不再感受，不再移動；
在她腳與頭二處
各躺著一個奴隸服侍著她，
　二者的屍骨與她的一樣枯白。

試問她是一位高貴的女仕，
深愛這世上的虛榮
　及愚蠢的浮華？
或是擁有所有天賦中
最貴重及最難得的氣質，
　像基督徒的仁愛、恭順及謙遜？

誰會告訴我們？大家都保持沉默；
對我們所提出的簡單問題，
　那些既無怒意也無驕意的人，
他們雙頰不露臉色；
而即使睡在她身邊的人，
　也不會揭穿這祕密。

# In the Churchyard at Cambridge (Cont'd,)

Hereafter?--And do you think to look
On the terrible pages of that Book
   To find her failings, faults, and errors?
Ah, you will then have other cares,
In your own short-comings and despairs,
   In your own secret sins and terrors!

# 劍橋的墓地裡（續）

今後呢？你是否會想看看
功罪簿上那些可怕的記載，
　　來發現她的弱點、缺陷及錯誤？
啊，那末你會另外擔心
自己的短處及絕望，
　　自己的私慾及恐懼！

# Inscription
# For Mayre's Heights, Fredericksburg
## —Herman Melville (1819-1891)

To them who crossed the flood

And climbed the hill, with eyes

Upon the heavenly flag intent,

And through the deathful tumult went

Even unto death: to them this Stone –

Erect, where they were overthrown –

Of more than victory the monument.


# Four Ducks on a Pond
## —William Allingham (1824-1889)

Four ducks on a pond,

A grass bank beyond,

The blue sky of spring,

White clouds on the wing;

What a little thing

To remember for years  –

To remember with tears.

# 碑文
## 為弗雷德里克斯堡之瑪莉高地而作
### ——赫爾曼・梅爾維爾（1819-1891）

汝等涉水攀山丘，
緊隨空中之旗幟，
出入混戰冒生死。
謹以此碑獻與汝，
碑立兵倒落敗處，
勝仗不敵紀念碑。


# 塘上四鴨
### ——威廉・阿林漢姆（1824-1889）

四隻鴨子泛塘上，
青蔥堤岸在遠方，
晴空蔚藍春色天，
白雲悠悠在飄揚；
就是這芝麻瑣事
年來使我不能忘—
每逢想起就流淚。

# Memory
## —Thomas Bailey Aldrich (1836-1907)

My mind lets go a thousand things
Like dates of wars and deaths of kings,
And yet recalls the very hour –
'T was noon by yonder village tower,
And on the last blue noon in May –
The wind came briskly up this way,
Crisping the brook beside the road;
Then, pausing here, set down its load
Of pine-scents, and shook listlessly
Two petals from that wild-rose tree.

# 記憶
## ——湯瑪斯・貝雷・阿爾曲奇（1836-1907）

我心中不計較千思萬緒，
諸如戰爭的日子及君王之薨歿，
但仍記得那一刻 —
那是五月最後的一個晴午，
在村莊遠處的一個鐘樓處 —
風輕快地朝此吹來，
吹皺路旁的溪水；
然後稍停，留下
滿簍松香，徐徐的將二片花瓣，
從野玫瑰樹上吹落下來。

# Somebody's Darling
## —Marie Ravenel de la Coste (1840?-1909?)

Into a ward of the whitewashed walls,
    Where the dead and the dying lay
Wounded by bayonets, shells, and balls,
    Somebody's darling was borne one day.
Somebody's darling – so young and so brave
    Wearing still on his pale, sweet face –
Soon to be hid by the dust of the grave –
    The lingering light of his boyhood's grace.

# 人家的心上人
## ——瑪麗·拉維內爾德拉斯科斯特（1840?-1909?）

進入粉刷成白色的病房，

　　那裡躺著被刺傷，受彈傷及砲傷而死

以及奄奄一息的人。

　　人家的孩子一天變成心上人。

人家的心上人 — 如此年輕又勇敢，

　　在他蒼白及可愛的臉上，

少年風度的光彩猶存，

　　不久即將被墳土所掩。

# Somebody's Darling (Cont'd.)

Matted and damp are the curls of gold
    Kissing the snow of that fair young brow,
Pale are the lips of delicate mould –
    Somebody's darling is dying now.
Back from the beautiful, blue-veined face
    Brush every wandering silken thread,
Cross his hands as a sign of grace –
    Somebody's darling is still and dead.

Kiss him once for somebody's sake,
    Murmur a prayer, soft and low,
One bright curl from the cluster take –
    They were somebody's pride, you know.
Somebody's hand has rested there:
    Was it a mother's, soft and white?
And have the lips of a sister fair
    Been baptized in those waves of light?

# 人家的心上人（續）

捲的金髮，濕又亂，
　　緊貼著白皙的額頭，美而年輕，
嘴唇的形狀優美而蒼白，
　　人家的心上人已在彌留中。
將他雜亂的細髮全部梳向
　　漂亮而帶青筋的臉後，
使他雙手交叉作感恩的標誌—
　　人家的心上人已僵死。

讓我替人家吻他一下，
　　輕而低聲地喃喃祈禱，
從他束髮中取出一根光亮的捲髮，
　　要曉得，人家以他的捲髮為榮。
一隻柔軟且潔白的手放在他身上：
　　那是母親的手？
漂亮妹妹的雙唇，
　　可曾在他金髮的光波中受過洗禮？

# Somebody's Darling (Cont'd.)

God knows best. He was somebody's love:
    Somebody's heart enshrined him there:
Somebody wafted his name above,
    Night and morn, on the wings of prayer.
Somebody wept when he marched away,
    Looking so handsome, brave and grand;
Somebody's kiss on his forehead lay,
    Somebody clung to his parting hand.

Somebody's watching and waiting for him,
    Yearning to hold him again to her heart; –
There he lies – with the blue eyes dim,
    And smiling, child-like lips apart.
Tenderly bury the fair young dead,
    Pausing to drop on his grave a tear:
Carve on the wooden slab at his head
    *Somebody's darling lies buried here.*

# 人家的心上人（續）

上帝最清楚。他曾是人家的心上人：
　　人家的心中珍藏著他：
從早到晚，人家乘著祈禱的雙翅，
　　在空中傳喚他的名字。
在他急行而去的那一刻，人家哭了，
　　他看來是如此的英俊，勇敢及崇高：
人家吻了一下他的前額，
　　緊握著他即將離開的手。

人家注視著他，等著他，
　　渴望再將他摟在她的胸前；一
他躺在那裡，碧藍的眼睛暗淡無光，
　　仍然笑著，像小孩似的張著口。
我親切地將這英俊的少年埋了，
　　逗留在他的墓上，一灑同情之淚：
在靠頭處的厚木板上為他刻著：
　　「人家的心上人葬於此。」

# Epitaph on an Army of Mercenaries
## —A.E. Houseman[1] (1859-1936)

These, in the day when heaven was falling,

　The hour when earth's foundations fled,

Followed their mercenary calling

　And took their wages and are dead.


Their shoulders held the sky suspended;

　They stood, and earth's foundations stay;

What God abandoned, these defended,

　And saved the sum of things for pay.

---

[1]　全名為Alfred Edward Housman.

# 雇傭軍的墓誌銘
## ——阿爾弗雷德‧愛德華‧豪斯曼（1859-1936）

當天堂要塌下的那天，
　　地層快崩塌的時刻，
他們響應雇傭軍的號召
　　賺得薪餉而成仁。

他們頂天立地；
　　他們之屹立使地基保存；
上帝所唾棄的、皆由他們來護衛，
　　祇為保存萬物而接受工資。

# Easter
## —Geoffrey Anketell Studdert-Kennedy (1883-1929)

There was rapture of spring in the morning
   When we told our love in the wood,
For you were the spring in my heart, dear lad.
   And I vow that my life was good.
But there's winter of war in the evening,
   And lowering clouds overhead,
There's wailing of wind in the chimney-nook,
   And I vow that my life lies dead.
For the sun may shine on the meadow lanes
   And the dog-rose bloom in the lanes,
But I 've only weeds in my garden, lad,
   Wild weeds that are rank with rains.

One solace there is for me, sweet but faint,
   As it floats on the wind of the years,
A whisper that spring is the last true thing
   And that triumph is born of tears.
It comes from a garden of other days,
   And an echoing voice that cries,
"Behold I am alive for evermore,
   And in Me shall the dead arise."

# 復活節
## ──傑佛瑞・安克泰爾・斯塔德特－甘迺迪
## （1883-1929）

早晨，當我們在林中私語，
　春天有它迷人之處，
因為，親愛的孩子，你是我心中的春天。
　我發誓過去的生活完滿。
但冬天的傍晚仍有戰事，
　頭上烏雲漸漸低沉，
煙囪角上風在嗚咽，
　我保證我的生命奄奄一息。
太陽許是照落在草地
　及巷旁綻開的犬玫瑰上，
但孩子，我園中只有野草，
　那雨後蕪生漫長的野草。

我只有一個甜蜜但隱約的慰藉，
　它隨著歲月的飛馳而飄動，
是一個春天畢竟會來的輕呼，
　一個榮耀生來就是痛苦的輕呼。
它來自將來的花園，
　是繚曲撕喊的迴響，
「瞧，我活得更久，
　死者在我心中復活。」

# Dulce et Decorum Est
## —Wilfred Owen (1893-1918)

Bent double, like old beggars under sacks,

Knock-kneed, coughing like hags, we cursed through sludge ,

Till on the hunting flares we turned our backs

And towards our distant rest began to trudge.

Men marched asleep. Many had lost their boots

But limped on, blood-shod. All went lame; all blind;

Drunk with fatigue; dead even to the hoots

Of tired, outstripped Five-Nines that dropped behind.

Gas! Gas! Quick, boys! – An ecstasy of fumbling,

Fitting the clumsy helmets just in time;

But someone still was yelling out and stumbling

And flound'ring like a man in fire or lime …

Dim, through the misty panes and thick green light,

As under a green sea, I saw him drowning.

# 以身殉國
## ——維爾浮萊德·歐文（1893-1918）

我們深彎著腰，像被壓在袋子下的老乞丐，
跌跌撞撞，邊走邊咳像醜老太婆，我們詛咒著越過爛泥，
直到在要命的砲火下，才轉身
開始朝遠方的歇息處艱步而行。
士兵們睡著行軍。很多掉了靴子
但仍跛足，滿腳裹血而行。大家都變成瘸子；成了瞎子；
飽嚐疲乏；甚至不顧
身後口徑5.9英吋的沈重砲聲
毒氣！毒氣！趕快，弟兄們 —— 一陣瘋狂的摸索，
及時調整笨重的鋼盔；
但仍有人在大聲喊叫，踉蹌
掙扎，像陷入火燄或毒煙中⋯⋯
透過濛霧的鏡片及深綠的光線，
暗得像在綠色的海水下，我看他漸漸沉沒。

# Dulce et Decorum Est (Cont'd.)

In all my dreams, before my helpless sight,
He plunges at me, guttering, choking, drowning.

If in some smothering dreams you could pace
Behind the wagon that we flung him in,
And watch the white eyes writhing in his face,
His hanging face, like a devil's sick of sin;
If you could hear, at every jolt, the blood
Come gargling from the froth-corrupted lungs,
Obscene as cancer, bitter as the cud
Of vile, incurable sores on innocent tongues, –
My friend, you would not tell with such high zest
To children ardent for some desperate glory,
The old Lie: Dulce et decorum est
 pro patria mori.[1]

---

[1] "Dulce et decorum est pro patria mori"此句出自羅馬詩人賀拉斯之頌歌(*Horace's Odes*) (III.2.13),英文的意思是:"It is sweet and fitting to die for one's fatherland."

# 以身殉國（續）

恍惚中，在我無奈的眼前
他突然倒向我，一邊淌口水，一邊嗆著，漸漸的撐不住了。

假定在令人窒息的夢中，你能緊跟在
他被扔上去的那輪馬車後面，
注視他那瞪白的眼在臉上痛苦地扭動，
及那搖晃的臉，連魔鬼也感到厭惡；
再如，車子每次顛動，你能從他受氣泡腐蝕的肺裡
聽到喉中咯咯的吐血聲，
像腫瘤般令人可憎，像痛苦地反覆咀嚼著
留在那無辜舌上髒而不治的潰瘍，—
那末，朋友，對那些急切熱衷於榮耀的孩子們，
你再不會高度熱誠地告訴
他們那則過氣的謊話：
「為國捐軀是受人喜愛且正當的。」

# 附錄（Appendix）
## ——作品一覽表（A List of Publications at a Glance）

## Books

1. *Guide to Legal Citation: A Canadian Perspective in Common Law Provinces* (Toronto, De Boo, International Thompson Ltd.,1984).
2. *Guide to Legal Citation and Sources of Citation Aid: A Canadian Perspective*, 2<sup>nd</sup> ed. (Toronto, De Boo, International Thompson Ltd., 1988).

## Law journal articles

1. "The Law of Citation and Citation of Law" (1986), 10:1 *Dalhousie Law Journal* 124-134.
2. "The Boundary Question in Space Law" (1973), 6 *Ottawa Law Review* 266-276.

## Newspaper articles

I was a regular contributor to the Commentary column of the *Taipei Journal* (formerly the *Free China Journal*) published by the Information Office of the Government of the Republic of China (Taiwan). The *Journal* was and has been a leading source of information concerning contemporary issues between Taiwan and the Mainland China. All articles listed below were written under my pen names, Xavier Teng or Charles S. Tam.

1. "A Man First, Then Chinese: Taiwan's Case for the U.N." (November 4, 1994), at 6.

2. "On the Harm in Unification with Communist Mainland" (April 28, 1995), at 6.

3. "What's Wrong at the Outset Cannot Have a Legal Descent" (May 26, 1995), at 6.

4. "A Fearless UN Would Heed Its Own Words on Equality" (September 22, 1995), at 6.

5. "Reunification Transcends Self-interest of Any Party" (January 26, 1996), at 6.

6. "On the Spirit of a People: In Witness of the Taiwan Experience" (March 22, 1996), at 1-2.

7. "Democracy, Unification: Ideas That Get on Just Fine" (May 10,1996), at 6.

8. "Independence Won't Stand as Basic Text of Separation" (August 30, 1996), at 6.

9. "Peking's Sovereignty Myth Denies UN Right to Millions" (October 5, 1996), at 6.

10. "Reality of a Divided China Calls for New Political View" (September 5, 1997), at 6.

11. "From an Ounce of Generosity to a Ton of Lasting Friendship" (May 15, 1998), at 6.

12. "This 'National Unity' Coin Shows Two Different Sides" (March 13, 1998), at 6.

13. "Does the Irish Settlement Hold a Lesson for Peking?" (August 14, 1998), at 6.

14. "Canadian Court's Decision: Precept for Chinese Unity" (October 9, 1998), at 6.

15. "Upholding a Moral Standard for the Honest and Innocent" (September 10, 1999), at 6.

16. "The Misfortunes of Nationalism" (January 14, 2000), at 6.

17. "Building Unity upon Diversity" (May 5, 2000), at 6.

18. "Changes Come from the People" (September 16, 2000), at 6.

19. "Chréstien Criticizes Rights Record" (March 30, 2001), at 6.

## Book reviews

1. Bank's *Using a Law Library* (1972), 50 *Canadian Bar Review* 691-694.

2. Matte's *Aerospace Law* (1978), 10 *Ottawa Law Review* 224-227.

3. *Annals of Air and Space Law* (1978), 10 *Ottawa Law Review* 467-471.

4. *Smith's Communications via Satellites* (1979), 57 *Canadian Bar Review* 186-188.

5. Matte's *Legal Implications of Remote Sensing from Outer Space* (1979), 25 *McGill Law Journal* 129-134.

6. Matte's *Space Policy and Programs Today and Tomorrow: The Vanishing Duopole* (1981), 59 *Canadian Bar Review* 619-622.

7. Bieber's *Dictionary of Current American Legal Citations* (1983), 15 *Ottawa Law Review* 512-513.

8. Matte's *Aerospace Law: Communications Satellites* (1985), 17 *Ottawa Law Review* 451-453.

9. "Unification and UN Denial: Tough Job Made Harder Yet," being a book review on *Divided Dynamism: The Diplomacy of Separate Nations: Germany, Korea, China,* by John J. Metzler (University Press of America, 1996), *Free China Journal* (January 17, 1997), at 6.

# 中文部分
## （除少數幾篇用真名外，其他皆以筆名「重嘉」發表）

1. 〈「華沙公約」有關空難事件損害賠償問題之規定〉刊《中國一周》第936期（民國五十七年四月一日），頁17-18。

2. 〈太空法上若干僵持問題之分析〉刊《法學叢刊》第四卷第四期（民國五十八年十月）頁66-74。

3. 〈失落的一群〉刊《海外學人》第165期（民國五十九年二月五日），頁71。

4. 〈河畔之晨〉刊於古蒙仁主編之《美的迴響》（民國七十六年），頁206-208。原載《中央日報海外版》（民國七十五年九月十七日），第四版。

5. 〈夢中的合歡山〉刊《海外學人》第189期（民國七十七年四月三日），頁63。

6. 〈人生小語〉刊《中央日報黃河版》（民國八十一年七月九日），第十六版。

7. 〈又見國旗〉刊《中央日報海外版》（民國八十一年十一月十二日），副刊版。

8. 〈生活數語〉刊《中央日報海外版》（民國八十二年二月十二日），第八版。

9. 〈周末的小天使〉刊《海光報》（民國八十二年十月十五日），第三版。

10. 〈從海外看重返聯合國〉刊《中央日報海外版》（民國八十二年十二月十五日）。

11. 〈古玩家的情懷〉刊《中央日報海外版》（民國八十三年十二月六日），第十一版。

12.〈從「芋仔」到「番薯」引發的省思〉刊《中央日報海外版》（民國八十四年二月二十五日）。

13.〈江波舞影，如柳隨風〉刊《中央日報海外版》（民國八十四年三月十日），第六版。

14.〈姓氏之煩惱〉刊《宏觀報》（民國八十四年八月一日），第七版。

15.〈天上人間，何人堪寄？〉刊《中央日報海外版》（民國八十五年一月二十三日），第七版。

16.〈五十年前的諾言〉刊《中央日報海外版》（民國八十六年三月二十四日），副刊版。

17.〈兩地茫茫未了情〉刊《宏觀報》（民國八十六年十一月二十六日），第七版。

18.〈也談自然寫作〉刊《宏觀報》（民國八十七年六月十八日），第八版。

19.〈生隨夢散〉刊《海外學人》第308期（民國八十九年五月），頁52。

20.《全民英檢中高級作文指南》台北：秀威資訊科技股份有限公司，民國九十五年。

國家圖書館出版品預行編目

悠閒自得：中英文詩詞選集 / 唐清世作. -- 臺
　北市：致出版, 2019.08
　　面；　公分
　中英對照
　ISBN 978-986-97897-2-1(平裝)

813.1　　　　　　　　　　108011435

# 悠閒自得
## ──中英文詩詞選集

作　　者／唐清世

出版策劃／致出版

製作銷售／秀威資訊科技股份有限公司

　　　　　114 台北市內湖區瑞光路76巷69號2樓

　　　　　電話：+886-2-2796-3638

　　　　　傳真：+886-2-2796-1377

網路訂購／秀威書店：https://store.showwe.tw

　　　　　博客來網路書店：http://www.books.com.tw

　　　　　三民網路書店：http://www.m.sanmin.com.tw

　　　　　金石堂網路書店：http://www.kingstone.com.tw

　　　　　讀冊生活：http://www.taaze.tw

出版日期／2019年8月　　　定價／350元

## 致　出　版
向出版者致敬